A Cab Called Reliable

Patti Kim

A Cab Called Reliable

a novel

St. Martin's Griffin New York

To my mother and father

I am grateful to my teachers at the University of Maryland: John Auchard, Michael Collier, Joyce Kornblatt, Reginald McKnight, Glenn Moomau, and Jack Salamanca.

If not for the friends at Global Missions Church and Cedar Ridge Community Church, I would be a miserable and lonely soul.

Design by Songhee Kim

The photographs in Chapter 10 are for the uses of fiction and should not be considered as fiction from life.

Library of Congress Cataloging-in-Publication Data

Kim, Patti.
A cab called Reliable / Patti Kim.
p. cm.
ISBN 0-312-19030-1
1. Korean American families—Fiction. 2. Korean Americans—Fiction. I. Title.
PS3561.I4146C33 1997
813'.54—dc21 97-7021
CIP

First St. Martin's Griffin Edition: July 1998

10 9 8 7 6 5 4 3 2 1

1

Our apartment on Burning Rock Court was two blocks away from Sherwood Elementary School. When I started third grade, my mother had told me that I had better know by heart the names of every street I had to walk along and across, or else I would remain forever missing because she had no clue where to go look for a nine-year-old girl stupid enough to lose her way in Arlington, Virginia. She said this place was nothing like Pusan.

In Pusan, my mother, father, little brother, and I used to live in a room behind a grocery store owned by my best friend's mother. Na-Ri and I used to make mud pies, jump rope, bang pots against pans, and sing jingles in front of her mother's store. Our favorite was for *Boo-Rah-Boh* ice cream cones. It went something like this: *Let's meet at noon for a Boo-Rah-Boh cone. We have to meet at noon for a Boo-Rah-Boh cone. No matter how the day goes, let's meet for a Boo-Rah-Boh cone.* I missed those cones. I missed Na-Ri.

A school bus screeched to a halt at the intersection of Wilson Boulevard and Oliver Lane. The crossing guard ushered me off the curb of the sidewalk. I looked left, right, left, crossed Oliver, tried hard to forget the ice cream cones, and practiced reciting the Pledge of Allegiance because Miss Washburn, my third-grade teacher, had chosen me to lead the rest of the class into the pledge for the next three mornings. Everyone thought it such an honor to stand in front of the class next to Miss Washburn's big brown desk, place their right hand upon their heart, and say "I pledge . . ." while the rest followed. But I dreaded it. I could never remember which words came after " . . . to the flag of the United States of America." Miss Washburn would surely be disappointed to find out I had been mumbling the whole time. I did not want to disappoint my teacher. I liked Miss Washburn. She had long brown hair with ends that curled into the shape of sixes. She wore lavender dresses that flowed when she strolled up and down the aisles. She played the piano and taught us songs about purple mountains and shining seas. She was nothing like my second-grade teacher, who had crooked teeth and called me Ann, Ann, Ann. If I had been older then, I would have politely told her that my name was not Ann. My name was pronounced like the sound one made after drinking iced lemonade on a hot day or when one began to understand why two plus two equals four. AH. My name is Ahn Joo. Like the "a" sound in "far." Far. The A with the two dots over it. Look it up in the dictionary. Like Aida. Ave Maria. Awabi.

While waiting for cars to pass on Thayer Street, the crossing guard asked me where I was from. When I answered her, she said she had a friend who was from that very same country. Then she asked me how long I had lived in America. "Two years," I said, and held up my two fingers. She smiled, nodded, and let me pass.

A group of older girls walked by me. The tallest of the four wore bright yellow tights and shiny black shoes. She was giggling and talking about boys. They hurried down the street toward the ABC Drug Store, where they would probably buy strawberry-flavored lip gloss, bubble gum, and fashion magazines.

Before turning onto my street, I waited to see if the girls did go into the ABC. I clapped my hands in triumph as I watched them run across the parking lot and disappear through the double doors.

I turned onto Burning Rock Court and skipped the rest of the way home, keeping an eye on the cracks in the sidewalk. Dandelions grew out of them. I stopped to pick a bunch. Then from a distance, I heard my little brother crying. I looked up and saw that he was being carried by my mother into a cab. She was wearing her brown-and-white polka-dotted skirt that clung to her thighs. She took long strides away from our home into the cab and thumped shut the door. Hiding behind a tree, I counted the dandelions in my hand. There were only four. When I heard the approaching car, I looked up to see my mother's stony face behind the half-opened window of a sky blue cab with "RELIABLE" written on the door.

The milk from the broken flower stems dripped down my wrist. I quickly licked it, remembering something my mother told me about dandelion milk being good for nervous stomachs. She also once said that it was wicked for a child to cry in public. She had pointed out to me a little black girl crying in a shopping cart at Pershing Market and said that the girl was a big show-off, bragging to the whole world what little control her mother had over her. My little brother often cried in public, but I was told Min Joo was special.

As I walked toward our apartment building with the black door marked "3501," I passed the parking spaces; the STOP sign that was missing its capital S; windows with blinds and without blinds, with curtains and without curtains; the broken swings at Burning Rock Court; Boris's apartment, which always smelled of garlic and onions; Kavitha's apartment, which smelled of dirty rags; the patch of weeds we cooked up meals for our brothers in; the bench we turned into a house with a sheet and two branches; and the white tree I sprained my wrist against running to first base. Last summer Kavitha's father sat underneath that white tree and performed magic tricks with his cigarette. He looked like a brown skeleton, tall and bald, and wore tattered pants held by a rope and no shoes. His toes were long. His feet were dusty. He looked to me like a man who while walking across the Sahara Desert decided to take a rest in the shade of our tree. My favorite of his tricks, which I called "The Living Ashtray," was when he would flick his cigarette ashes back onto his tongue with his lower lip. No hands. I saw the ashes land on his tongue. I saw him swallow them, too. I thought it was amazing that a man could carry ashes in his body, and when I told my mother about it, she said to stay away from Kavitha and her family because those things were works of demons.

I walked past the tree with a different feeling from the one I had last summer or even yesterday walking home from school. What a silly monkey I must have been to laugh, clap, and sing along with the other children. What a stupid girl I must have been to braid blades of grass into bracelets, necklaces, and engagement rings.

As I climbed the stairs to the second floor, I wondered where RELIABLE might be.

I pressed my ear against the neighbor's door. I listened for the flute I had once heard back in December when I knocked for my father, who wanted to give the American woman next door a gift for the holidays. "Do you want a Korean calendar?" I had asked. But there was now no sound of flutes, only the sound of my breathing and my footsteps.

Our door was not locked. I turned the knob, walked inside, sat down next to my father's boots, and began to cry, remembering the expression on my mother's face. She looked as if I were the last thing on her mind. I had seen that expression before. She wore that scary you-mean-nothing-to-me look on her face whenever she and my father fought.

I was alone in the apartment, but there, right there, I could see my mother sitting in front of the television. I could have sworn she was there. She was ironing my father's dress shirt. It was a Sunday morning, and she was getting us ready for church—the New Covenant Korean Church. An hour and a half away, but my mother woke us up and made us go every Sunday. My Sunday School teacher's name was Howard. He had orange hair, freckles, and wore a shirt that had yellow, green, red, and orange parrots painted on it. He taught us that the devil was a beautiful lying snake and that God spoke through donkeys.

My mother, with her ironing quilt laid out in front of her, pressed my father's collar, cuffs, front side, back side, right sleeve, left sleeve, and told me to pull my dress down, pull my socks up, tuck my hair behind my ears, and wake up Min Joo and Father. Min Joo was combing his hair in the bathroom. Father still slept.

My mother was wearing a two-piece dress. It was pink, with tiny black roses lined up in columns and rows. Her hair was tied in a braided bun. Fake diamond earrings with dangling blue teardrop stones. After pressing my father's shirt, she folded the quilt and pushed it underneath the sewing machine. The iron, still hot and propped up, stood next to the door. On the doorknob hung my father's dress shirt.

I crossed my legs. I waited near the shoes. Min Joo's wet hair was parted down the middle. When he sat next to me, I smelled shampoo. I told him he didn't wash it all out. "Your hair's still soapy. Your hair's going to fall out."

Min Joo shrugged his shoulders, pressed his elbows onto his knees, rested his chin in the palms of his hands, and told me that our father was still sleeping.

"You should've woken him up," I said. "You know what's going to happen, don't you? Don't you?"

I should have woken him up. *I* should have swung open his door, stomped across the room, pulled up the blinds, turned him onto his back, shaken his shoulders, jumped on the bed, pulled the blanket to the floor, clanged pot lids against each other, and screamed in his ear that Mother was coming with the back scratcher.

Mother came.

Is this woman crazy? Get the hell off of me!

You're not going to wake up? You're still smelling of vodka. I wash and iron your clothes until my tongue falls out, and you stink it up with vodka and cigarettes. What is this smell? What is it?

You're making too much noise. I'm getting up. Stop screaming.

Get out of my bed!

I'm getting out.

What have I done wrong? What is it? Why do you treat me like this? You can't make me live like a dog.

You're making too much noise. I'm getting up.

Lying coward. Where were you last night?

Shut up, crazy begging bitch.

I'm crazy. I'm crazy! Min Joo-yah, Ahn Joo-yah, your mother is crazy. Come in and smell your father's breath. Listen to your crazy mother and smell your father's breath. Smell his clothes. Smell them and ask him where he's been all night.

I'm getting up.

Korea or America, you're just the same. No change. No change.

You're making too much noise.

Where are you going? Are you still drunk? The bathroom's over there. Get in the shower. Take a shower, you coward.

Leave me alone. I'm getting a drink.

There were pink streaks on my father's arm. His pajama pants hung low underneath his belly. He combed his hair with his fingers and walked toward the kitchen. My mother followed.

Again? You're drinking in the morning?

Water, bitch. I'm getting water. Leave me alone.

Drink in the shower.

Are you not going to shut your mouth? Do you want me to smack it shut?

My father swung his arm back and covered his ears. My mother followed him, but stopped. She stopped, turned, picked up the iron, and struck my father on the back of his head. He stopped, gripped the back of a chair, shook his head, then walked on. He got water from the refrigerator and drank it. Min Joo's face was buried in his lap; his head wrapped up with his arms. Mother was breathing heavily. She coiled the cord around the iron and laid it on its side on top of the folded quilt. As she walked to the bedroom, she pulled her earrings off. Clutching them in her hand, she turned around, waved her fist in the air, and with the scary expression on her face, she told my father he would live with regret for the rest of his life. My mother threw her earrings on the dresser and shut the door.

The apartment was quiet. I was alone. I stopped crying.

On the kitchen table was a white box with a red ribbon tied around it. On the top right corner was written *Cho, Ahn Joo* in Korean. Inside were four perfect little white-frosted square cakes, the kind I had seen only through bakery windows and in storybooks where girls wore yellow bows with matching yellow aprons and had parties with cake and tea. Two of my cakes were decorated with pink ribbons and two with pineapples, and there was a note tucked between the two kinds. In Korean, my mother had written to tell me that the cakes were for me and to eat them slowly and deliciously and wait with patience because she would come back to get me. With my thumb and middle finger I held a piece of cake to my mouth, smiled, and wondered why I had almost cried minutes ago, forgetting that I had seen how rushed, determined, scary, and secretive my mother looked with Min Joo in her arms as she entered the cab that looked ready to drive off far away. I ate all four pieces and licked the wax paper that lined the bottom of the box. I decided to keep the white box to carry my most important things in for when my mother came back to take me to where she, Min Joo, and I would secretly live.

I put in the box the four dollars in change I had saved from milk money I had not used because milk made my stomach turn; the lipstick called Devon Rose #260 I had stolen from my second-grade teacher's purse because I thought such a person did not deserve to wear such a beautiful color; a poem about my mother that I had written in brown Magic Marker called "Tears in the Toilet"; and the rock Boris had tossed up my pant leg during recess. I removed my pillow and stuffed the empty pillowcase with my spelling book because I needed to know how to spell wherever I went; my favorite yellow dress, with buttons the shape of stars; clean underwear, white socks, and the red mittens my grandmother had knitted for me and sent all the way from Pusan in a box full of dried kelp, dried red peppers, and dried anchovies.

Then I placed my box and pillowcase near the door

and sat on the radiator underneath the window, looking out for a blue cab with RELIABLE written on the door. I counted the cars that drove by and took in the scene at Burning Rock Court as if for the very last time.

Removed from everything that had gone on the night before and the night before and the night before, I felt that the girl who had seen her mother throw a hot iron at her father because he smelled of liquor, perfume, smoke, and urine again, who had seen her father bounce her mother's head on and off the refrigerator door calling her a begging bitch because she mentioned returning to Korea again, who had seen the dark blue print of her father's hand around her brother's neck, who had felt the same large hand remain seconds too long on her own bottom as he patted her for being a good girl and then on her stomach as he rubbed her indigestion away—that girl was no longer me. That girl would have been standing in front of a mirror reciting the Pledge of Allegiance. But I was here with my most important things packed and ready to be taken to the secret place where only mothers, daughters, and little brothers were allowed.

I began to hum a tune my mother once taught me. I did not know the words to the song, but I remembered it was about a girl who lived in the country and was watching her older brother ride a horse on the road to the city. When his figure became as small as the size of her thumb, she returned to the house and stared out the window. She was sad, but full of hope because her brother had promised to return soon with a pair of silk slippers.

As I saw the sky changing colors, I began to panic because hours had already gone by and my mother had not yet come for me. I panicked, thinking she had forgotten about me or had somehow found out about all the naughty things I had said and done to torture Min Joo and decided it would be best to leave me with my father. I prayed Min Joo did not tell her how I carried him on my shoulders and dropped him on the floor, how I held down his head in our bathwater, how I told him to brush his teeth with soap, how I told him Mother and I had found him underneath a bridge in a Korean village where lepers lived. If my mother knew these things, she would surely never return for me, and my father would find me here with my most important things and never ever let me leave.

With my mother's note in hand, I took my belongings outside. Waiting on the bench, I prayed that Min Joo, wherever he was, would be crying, because my brother was not able to cry and speak at the same time.

From across the court, Boris Bulber saw me sitting on the bench and began limp-running toward me with a bag of corn chips. He was wearing a brown T-shirt and a pair of brown corduroys that were too tight and too short for him. Brown eyes, brown skin, brown hair. Everything on him seemed to match. I wondered if on a map, Portugal would also be the color brown.

He sat down next to me, twitched his good leg, and offered me a corn chip. I told him my stomach wasn't feeling good and I could throw up all over him any minute. He smiled, showing me the gap between his two front teeth, and told me I could come over and play because his mother was working at the motel today. She was a cleaning lady for the Madison Inn, which was the two-story white brick building with orange, yellow, green, and blue doors. It stood between Buckingham Theater and the Rose Garden Chinese Restaurant, right across the street from Pershing Market. I had seen Boris's mother come home from work before. She wore what looked to me like a nurse's uniform: white blouse, white skirt, white shoes, and two safety pins holding up the gray apron that covered her large breasts. The first time I saw her, she looked so important and professional that I decided when I grow up, I would like to be a cleaning lady at the Madison Inn.

"Boris, I can't play today. I'm moving," I said and pulled my things closer to me.

"Where're you moving?"

"To Hawaii."

"You're not coming to school tomorrow?"

"It's the last time you can see me."

"You can come over right now, can't you?" he asked. Looking at my things, he said, "You're not moving."

"My mother's coming to get me," I said.

"That's my window. You can look out," he said, pointing in that direction. "I'll give you my quarter."

Because Boris was the only boy who had ever kissed me, I told him I would come over and play with him, but only for five minutes because my mother was coming to get me any minute now. He pulled out a quarter from his pocket, put it in my hand, stood up, and told me to come on. With one arm around my box and the pillowcase slung over my other shoulder, I followed Boris to his apartment, where he would sit me on his lap and kiss me.

"Don't touch me. That's yucky," I said.

"If you like someone, you can touch them there," Boris said, putting his head on my shoulder. I sniffed into his curls, shrugged him off, and told him his head was making me cry because it smelled just like onions.

I stood up to look out the window. Parked in the center of the court was a white van, but there was no cab—blue, yellow, green, black, or any other color, with any sort of lettering on its door. I did not want to wait outside because it was getting dark and my father would see me with my things and make me stay with him forever. When Boris's mother came in through the door saying something to Boris in Portuguese, I tried hard to remember my mother's song, wondering if the country girl ever got her silk slippers in the end.

After seeing me at her window, Boris's mother walked into the kitchen telling the air it was natural and all right for a girl and boy to kiss as long as no one had a cough, sneeze, or sniffle. She filled a saucepan with water, placed it on the stove, and brought out four potatoes from the cabinet under the sink. While scrubbing them, she told me to stay and eat something because my head looked too big for my body. Skin and bones, she called me. On the television set was a framed photograph of Boris's father. He was smiling and waving, hello or good-bye, from the driver's seat of a truck. Poor Boris and his mother were still waiting for him to drive the truck back to Arlington from somewhere in Texas.

I told Boris's mother I needed to eat by the window because my mother was coming soon to get me. Boris told her we were moving to Hawaii. She did not believe me; nevertheless, she smiled and said that Hawaii was a beautiful place, and I was a lucky girl. Then she left me with my bowl of potatoes with butter and garlic at the windowsill while she and Boris ate at the table.

As I finished my food, I saw that the light of our apartment was turned on. My father must have come home. I asked Boris's mother for another bowl of potatoes because they were more delicious than anything I had ever eaten, and she gladly took my bowl and filled it. Before giving me a second helping, she wiped my mouth with a corner of her gray apron, and puckering her lips at me—the way lips are puckered at poor strays—she called me a sweet girl. I quickly finished the potatoes, took my bowl to the sink, slipped the spoon into my sleeve, gathered up my belongings, and thanked Boris's mother for a delicious dinner. I told Boris it was time for me to go because my mother was waiting.

Outside, I crawled into the azalea shrubs that grew near our building and with the spoon dug a hole deep enough to hide my box and pillowcase. If my father saw my things, he would point his middle finger at the box, tell me in that voice my mean and greedy grandfather used to open it up, and then, seeing the four dollars in change, he would pocket it. Reading my poem, he would know that I knew it was because of him my mother cried into the toilet. The rock he would throw out the window because rocks were dangerous weapons in the hands of children. Looking at the lipstick, he would tell me that eight-year-old girls with color on their faces grew up to be whores, and I would tell him I was already nine. But I would never tell my father about the note and the cakes that had been left for me.

When I walked into our apartment, I saw my father's back. He was looking out the window, with the telephone receiver held between his shoulder and ear. One hand held the phone; the other was moving a cigarette from his lips to his side, where he flicked the ashes onto the floor. My mother used to yell at him for that. I quietly shut the door, sat on the arm of the sofa, and listened to my father trying to ask Mina or Hyun-Joo or Whan's father or mother in a careful and polite way where his wife might be. My mother used to baby-sit for all of them.

"Yes, I know about that. She told me she would stop baby-sitting Mina," he said. Turning around, my father saw me and said with a smile, "You have to excuse me. She just came in." He set the telephone down on the air conditioner and walked toward me with his work boots still on his feet. He placed his large, open hand on top of my head, held it like a ball, then gently pushed it back so that he could take a good look at me while asking where I had been, and where my mother went.

"I played at Boris's house," I said.

"Where's your mother? Where's your brother?"

I shrugged my shoulders and told him Min Joo

wasn't in school all day; the door was locked when I came home, and with no place to go, I went over to Boris's. I told him Boris's mother gave me potatoes for dinner so I wasn't hungry at all. ·My father removed his hand and walked into the kitchen where he kept bottles on top of the refrigerator. I followed him. With a drink in hand, he went into the bathroom. Following him, I asked, "Where are they? Where are they?" As he washed his face with cold water, I squatted on the rim of the toilet seat and stopped asking where they might be. I watched him comb his hair back with his fingers, and thought that my father was a handsome man. After drying himself, he told me to get off the toilet, get out of the bathroom. When he shut the door, I pressed my ear against it and listened for my father's breathing. I held the knob ready to turn if the bathroom suddenly became silent.

I followed my father everywhere because I did not want him to disappear. I followed him to his bedroom, where he opened and shut the dresser drawers, checking for my mother's clothes. He sat on the bed and took off his work boots. He searched for his secret cigar box of emergency money that had been hidden in the closet. I followed him to my room, where in the dark he kicked my box of Magic Markers and threw my notebooks at the walls. He kicked the leg of my desk. He kicked the radiator. I followed him to the living room, where he turned the television on, drank some more, asked me if she said anything in the morning, and made phone calls. To one person he said, "Did Ahn Joo's mother mention anything about meeting you tomorrow?" To another, he called my mother a begging bitch, told the person she stole all of his emergency money and ran away, and when she returned, he would beat her to death.

I followed him to his room, where he sat on his bed and drank more. Lying next to him on my mother's side of the bed, I felt my eyes grow heavy with sleep. I did not want my father to disappear. Before closing my eyes, I placed a finger on his shirt and listened to my father drinking and smoking and thinking of what he would do to my poor mother when she came home to get me, and what my poor father would do when she started nagging again about his drinking, coming home late, not enough money to even feed the children whole milk, magazines of long-legged women that could have paid for his son and daughter's school lunch tickets for an entire month, why did you bring me to this awful country. If I hadn't married the likes of you, I wouldn't be washing someone else's dishes, delivering newspapers I can't read, looking after someone else's children. What kind of living is this? This is a dog's life. And you are a coward for running away from your father like a beaten dog. No wonder you are a drunk and a lousy father and husband—look at the family you learned from.

My father would return her words with a smack or a tight collar made by his hand around her neck. The collar would tighten and tighten, as she looked at him with her go-ahead-and-kill-me-I'm-ready-to-die-death-is-better-than-life-with-you look in her eyes.

As I fell asleep thinking of my mother's voice, I prayed that it would rain because Min Joo cried when it rained; but remembering that my things were buried outside, I changed my mind and asked God to stop the rain. I asked God to hurry up and return my mother to me. *Please, please, please hurry up,* I begged. I promised never to torture Min Joo ever again. I promised to be good. And if God was not able to hurry them home, I asked him to please show me where in the world RELIABLE might be.

2

The telephone rang. I answered it with a hello, waited for a response, asked who it was, then waited in silence. The person on the other end hung up, and I was certain she would call again because I was convinced it was my mother wanting to hear my breathing, my voice. The telephone rang again. This time, I answered it with a hello in Korean. When I heard quiet breathing, I called out: *"Mother, Mother, it's me, Ahn Joo. I'm here. I'm waiting. When will you come for me?"* But the voice at the other end belonged to a man. His name was Paul. He asked what language I was speaking, what country I was from, and if my mother or my father was home. He said my English was very good and he could tell from my voice that I had a pretty face. "You're pretty, aren't you?" he asked. I smiled and nodded. He asked my age, my school, my favorite color, my favorite time of day, my favorite ice cream flavor, television show, and holiday. He said he liked the way ice cream felt in his mouth, icy and creamy, and asked if I knew how good that felt. He asked if I had a boyfriend. He asked what I was wearing. When I told him a blue dress, he said to lift it up and touch the place between my legs.

3

Miss Washburn sat at her desk and ate spaghetti out of a blue plastic bowl. The rest of the class was outside for recess. She and Mrs. Martin took turns monitoring the third graders' recess time, and today was her day to have thirty-five minutes of quiet to herself. Sipping from the lid of her thermos, Miss Washburn looked up at me and asked why I wasn't playing outside with everyone else. I handed her a piece of paper on which I had printed the word RELIABLE in capital letters and asked her if she knew where it might be. She put down her drink, held the paper in both hands, tilted her head, squinted, leaned toward me, and explained that the word was not a noun. "A noun is a person, place, or thing. Reliable," she said, "is not a place, person, or thing. It's an adjective. Ahn Joo, do you remember what an adjective is?"

"Yes," I said, nodding.

"Can you tell me what it is?"

"A describing word. It describes a noun," I answered.

"Where did you see the word?" she asked, holding the paper up to me.

When I told her I had seen it on a cab, she smiled and said that it was very smart of me to write down words I did not know the meaning of. She explained that "Reliable" was probably the name of the cab company, and the reason they called it that was because they wanted their customers to know that their service was reliable or dependable or responsible or faithful or trustworthy. When I returned her explanation with a confused stare, she pushed her seat away from the desk, stood up, and pointing to her chair, said, "See this chair? It is reliable because I know it will not break when I sit on it. See?" Miss Washburn sat back down. She tapped the toes of her canvas sandals against the floor. Her fingers were spread out upon her lap. "Now, you tell me, Ahn Joo, what other things can be reliable."

Pointing my chin at her, I said, "You."

Miss Washburn put her hands together, smiled as if she had won a contest, took a breath, and leaned down to hug me. Her hair smelled like brand-new crayons. She then went to the back of the classroom, brought back to her desk the *Living Dictionary,* and read aloud to me the definition of the word: "Worthy of trust. That can be depended on. Worthy of being depended on or trusted. Reliable implies that a person or thing can safely be trusted and counted on to do or be what is expected, wanted, or needed." She closed the book, smiled, and asked if the word made sense to me. I nodded.

"Ahn Joo, why don't you do an exercise with the word. Why don't you do what we always do with new words?"

"You mean write them up and down?" I asked.

Miss Washburn in her singing voice said with excitement, "Yes, yes, write the word up and down, and think up others that start with the same letters."

Making lists was one of my teacher's most favorite

and important lessons. Each morning began with a list of things to do for the day, and each afternoon ended with a list of things to do for homework. She covered the walls of our classroom with rows and columns of rules like BE AT THE RIGHT PLACE AT THE RIGHT TIME and WALK—DO NOT RUN. She listed the fifty states of America in alphabetical order, with Alabama near the ceiling and Wyoming touching the floor.

I took back my piece of paper, politely thanked Miss Washburn, went to my seat in the fifth row, and for a few seconds put my stupid head down. RELIABLE was not a person, place, or thing. What was I thinking, trying to locate it on a map or atlas?

As Miss Washburn finished her bowl of spaghetti, I opened my notebook to a blank page, wrote the word up and down along the red margin, listed words that began with the letter R, then E, then L, then I, and became bored with the exercise. My teacher winked at me as she left the classroom to rinse out her empty bowl and fork. The sound of her footsteps faded down the hall. I tore the page out of my notebook, crinkled it up, and tossed the ball of paper into the wastebasket.

The wind blew in through the window and fluttered the corners of Miss Washburn's posters. Across the top of the chalkboard hung the long green strip of the alphabet. The white letters were written in perfect script. The arrows around all the curved lines showed us how to write in cursive, when to move and lift our pencils, and in which direction to take them. Take your pencil this way. Take it that way. I began to scribble in my notebook. I could hear the others playing outside. I imagined Judy and Kirk were trying to have sex in the forsythia shrubs.

"R is for rain," I wrote. "My little brother cried when it rained."

The bell rang. I put my pencil down and ran my fingers over the words with which I had filled two entire pages. The classroom smelled of oranges. There were peelings on Miss Washburn's desk. She was writing math problems on the chalkboard. I liked hearing the clean *tap, tap, tap* of the chalk against the board. I showed her my writing. She read the first page, took a seat, turned to the second, and looked up at me with proud eyes on the verge of tears. "Do you know how wonderful this is?" she asked. She wanted my permission to make a poster of my words to hang on the bulletin board. She said it was the most beautiful writing she had ever read.

The next morning, my words covered an entire bulletin board. Miss Washburn had labeled my writing "New Word of the Week." This was what I had written:

> *R is for rain. My little brother cried when it rained. I could depend on my brother to cry. A walnut formed on his chin. Tears fell down his cheeks. He cried winter, spring, summer, and fall. I never liked to hear him cry, but I miss it now. My little brother and mother went away. I miss them very much. I wish I could hear him cry again.*

E is for eat. I like to eat cupcakes. I could depend on them to make me happy. My mother used to make me fish cakes and rice cakes. I didn't like them because they tasted too salty and felt too slippery in my mouth. But if she made them for me right now, I would not mind. I would actually thank her and happily eat them.

L is for locusts. I could depend on them to visit every seventeen years. The noise they make fills the summer air. It keeps me company. No one can escape it.

I is for India. Kavitha and her family is from India. India is a country in Asia. I could depend on her because she is my friend. We like to make dandelion sandwiches for our brothers. She keeps all of my secrets.

A is for abba. *That's the Korean word for "father." That's also the Indian word for "father." I say it whenever I need him. I could depend on him. My father does not go away.*

B is for baby-sitter. My mother used to baby-sit Mina, Hyun-Joo, and Whan. The babies depended on her. She fed them water, rice, and soy sauce. She changed their diapers. She played with them. When they cried, she bounced them upon her lap. When they became sick, she placed her eye on their forehead to feel for the fever.

L is for love. My mother used to sing Korean love songs. One was about the love for a river. Another was about the love for a mountain. And another was about the love of a mother. She sang about chrysanthemums, barley fields, and whispering winds. She knew many songs by heart. But only one line to only one song was taught to me: "It's not love if you can't let me go."

E is for exit. I could depend on the red signs. They blink and reflect light. They hang above the main doors in Sherwood Elementary School. We can all depend on them to show us where to go at the end of the day, when the last bell ringalingalings.

Day after day, posters were made and hung all over the classroom walls. We learned the meanings to prima donna, martyr, festival, antepenultimate. . . . With each new poster, the words became longer.

When the last day of third grade came along, we signed our posters, rolled them up, and traded them. I took home Judy Davis's definition of the word "exotic." I thanked Miss Washburn, hugged her good-bye, and walked out of room 304 for the last time.

4

During silent reading, my book about volcanoes was propped up and opened on page sixteen. I sat in desk number six in the third row of Mr. Albert's fourth-grade class. My desk partners were falling asleep. Jason drooled onto his book about the Civil War. Our teacher sat in his recliner in the back of the classroom and read the sports page of his newspaper.

I laid my book down, turned the page, and smoothed my hand over the glossy pictures. I traced my thumb over the lava that poured out of the volcano's opening. I traced it down to my other hand, which was flattened at the bottom edge of the book. With the nail of my left index finger, I scratched a line across the center of my knuckles. Two inches. I told myself that there had to be two inches of water above the rice. My father's rice had to be sticky enough to stay on the tips of his chopsticks as he brought them to his lips. One night the rice was too watery, and he complained about having to use a spoon. He said he hadn't come all the way to America to lose his wife and son to a poor man's bowl of porridge. The night before, the rice had been too dry. Two nights before, I had forgotten to push the "on" button on the rice cooker, left it on "warm," and the grains simmered in the water and turned into hard rice cakes. My father had knuckled my head and told me to throw the entire pot away and that we would have to wait thirty more minutes for dinner. Thirty more minutes meant two more drinks.

As I watched Laurie get up from her seat to wash the blackboard, I told myself that tonight's rice had to be perfect. When I flattened my hand into the water, it had to cover all my fingers and its surface had to meet the center of my knuckles. The water had to end at the center of my knuckles.

Laurie placed the wet sponge underneath the green cardboard strip of the alphabet that was taped above the board and smoothed it down while gently squeezing out the water. She was underneath the letter D. To her left, the board had already dried an even black. To her right were chalk dust and numbers that hadn't been erased. After every three strokes, Laurie bent down, doused her sponge in the bucket of water, squeezed it dry, and started again.

I closed my volcano book, took out my notepad, and made a list of what needed to be done before my father came home from work. The *kimchi* needed to be sliced, the yellow radishes washed. A pot of water needed to be boiled with half a cup of dried anchovies, salt, and chopped green onions for the dumpling soup. I had to boil the dried corn to make tea, which would take at least two and a half hours. I decided to fry the last two eggs with baloney slices rather than hot dog slices because they were easier to cut, and they cooked faster. And the faster something cooked, the more time I would have to wash my father's corduroy and denim pants that he wore to work, to scrub the bathroom sink and tub after he washed, and to shake the dried dirt off his boots. Then I could quickly finish my homework and read if Hazel, Fiver, Speedwell, Pipkin, and the whole lot of them safely crossed the river on their journey to find a new home.

The bell rang. From the back of the room, Mr. Albert shouted, "Pop quiz tomorrow. Know Columbus and his three ships. What are they?" In unison, the class answered, *"Niña, Pinta, Santa María,"* and closed their books. As all the others packed their bags, placed their chairs on the tops of their desks, and ran to the door, I remained seated and bit my thumbnail, wondering if it was possible for one to discover a land that had already been found while trying to remember if there was enough cooking oil to fry the eggs.

Boris was asking Mr. Albert about long division; he didn't know which number went into which how many times and which number went under which and which got added or subtracted and what about the leftovers? While everyone else filed out of the room, Boris held up his math book to Mr. Albert. Our teacher stretched, went to the blackboard, worked out one problem for him. Then he told Boris he'd teach it again tomorrow. "You'll get it sooner or later," he said.

Boris nodded, dropped his math book in his bag, and made his way across the room. The keys on the right belt loop of his tan denim pants jingled as he limped toward the door.

I followed him down the hall past water fountains, classrooms, boys' and girls' bathrooms, and bulletin boards with borders of stapled tulips made of purple construction paper. As I walked past each classroom, I smelled glue and vinegar from the Easter egg dyes. At the end of the hall, a white rabbit cut out of butcher paper was pasted up with masking tape. The top of one of its pink ears reached the ceiling and the other drooped over its red eye. Its pink tail touched the floor. I smoothed my fingers over the center of the rabbit as I turned the corner. I matched my steps with Boris's. Right, left. Right, left. When I got close enough, I yanked his keys and giggled behind my fist. I turned, faced him, and with a bounce attending each step asked: "You still don't know long division?"

"Shut up, Ahn Joo," he said, and continued to *limp, clink, limp, clink* toward the swinging double doors that led to the stairs. The others in the hall gave Boris his space so that he could lift and drag his braced leg, then take a step with his good one without bumping into anyone. I followed him.

"I'm not a liar, Boris. I am moving to Hawaii," I said.

"You're a fake," he said.

His keys jingled clumsily as he quickened his wobble. His fists landed on the double doors and he leaned his chest in, swinging one open. As Boris held the left rail and limped down the stairs, I followed, skipping steps until I stood head to head with him.

"I'm not a fake. Everything just got postponed, that's all. What's your problem? I just wanted to help out. I got a check plus on my homework. I know how to do it. I'll show you, if you come over," I said.

"You come over," he said, as he took the last step and walked toward the exit.

I paused at the bottom of the stairs. At the end of the hall—past the glass doors of the main office, past the bench with its vinyl cushions and metal legs, past the two pay phones, past the display case of origami birds, boats, and flowers made by the first graders—stood four doors side by side underneath the electric red EXIT sign that hung from the ceiling. Boris was walking toward the fourth door with his right arm out and his elbow slightly bent, ready to push the metal bar that would take him outside.

Through the glass doors of the main office I saw the white clockface with a border of black numbers that fit snugly in the corner of the wall and ceiling. The clock hung over a square speaker—the big hand on the ten, the little hand on the two. The red hand, anchored in the center, patiently circled over the numbers. I scraped my heel against the edge of the last step. I pulled and twisted the top button of my orange sweater. The point of the red hand was reaching the twelve. As it floated over eleven, I ran toward Boris, leaned my back against the metal bar, and before pushing the door open, I said in his face, "I'll walk home with you. I'll come over. I'll help."

Boris smiled, his upper lip lifting to show his gums, and said, "I'm not paying you anything."

The cushions of Boris's green couch were scratchy. I could see Burning Rock Court through his window. I kept an eye out for my father's car. Boris's hands were very sweaty. He sat close to me. I placed my hands on his lap and told him to hold them. He placed one hand on top of mine. I sandwiched it between mine and rubbed it in circles as if I were rolling dough into balls. Quickly at first, then as I felt Boris's hand relax, his fingers feeling for mine, I slowed my circles until my hands barely moved. With his free hand, Boris formed a fist and rubbed it along the crack where his thigh met the cushions of the couch. He looked up, breathing heavily, and asked, "What'd you stop for?"

I shushed him and stroked his thumb with my forefinger. Around the top and into the crevice. As my thumb kneaded each of his knuckles, Boris closed his eyes, curled his back, and pressed his knees together. His nails were bitten. I played with the pinky, then the ring finger, middle, forefinger, and when I came to his thumb, I milked it and pulled it to my face and into my mouth. When I began to feel Boris's thumb move on its own, I let go of his hand and gently held his wrist.

Boris's eyelids fluttered. He tucked his lower lip into his mouth. Thinking that he was getting sick, I pulled out his thumb, wiped it on my sweater, returned it to his side, and said, "You look retarded."

"I'm not retarded," he said, and kissed me, pushing his tongue into my mouth.

I wanted to lie down on his couch and let him climb on top of me the way men climbed on top of women on TV. I wanted to tell him he was my one and only boyfriend and I wasn't ever going to move to Hawaii. Instead, I pushed him away, kicked his shin, told him to wake up, told him to get his book out fast because I didn't have time to fool around with a retarded and handicapped boy who didn't know his long division.

Even after four math problems, Boris couldn't straighten his back. His numbers, crooked and slanted, could barely be read on the page. As I divided five into two hundred six and six into four thousand nine and turned the remainders into fractions, Boris propped his elbow on his knees, pushed his thumb underneath his nose, and sniffed. I snatched his arm away from his face, stuck a pencil in his hand, told him to do the next problem and that he better not get it wrong.

"Kiss me, Ahn Joo," Boris said, as he fixed his narrowing eyes on my mouth. His lower lip hung.

I tilted my head to the right, blinked twice, leaned forward, and brushed my lips against his: right, left, up, and down, then planted them on his nose. When he pressed his opened mouth into mine, I cupped his cheeks in my hands, pulling him closer to me. The top of my nose looked blurry. Boris's eyelids were shut tight, his eyebrows knitted, his forehead scrunched. How stupid of Boris to keep his eyes closed. I studied the long crack that began at the ceiling, ran through a painting of a pond full of lilies, and ended as it met the cushions of the green couch. But I imagined the crack, crooked and uncertain, traveling down behind the couch onto the linoleum floor, through the swinging door that led to the kitchen, and finally ending underneath the breathing refrigerator.

While I let Boris breathe into my ear, I closed my eyes and counted my father's footsteps, heavy and tired. His knocks against the apartment door echoed in the hall. When I didn't come to the door with my usual greeting, my father would unlock it and let himself in, mumbling something about me sleeping too much after school. No red light on the rice maker. When he lifted the lid, no rice. No soup on the stove.

In the sink, dried orange juice on the sides of the glass. Dried rice and cereal stuck on the bowls. Wooden chopsticks and spoons. Dripping faucet. The table wasn't set with cups for the water, bowls for the rice, chopsticks and spoons on the right, folded napkins on the left, and last night's leftovers, slices of bean curd fried in egg with soy sauce and vinegar, in the center. When I heard my father shouting, *Wake up, what do you think nighttime is for?* I opened my eyes and saw the crack travel across the ceiling onto the opposite wall and across the floor, meeting the soles of my shoes. I sprang up, shook Boris's hand off my wrist, packed my school bag, and told Boris I had to go.

I kicked the couch and said, "Let go, Boris. I have to go immediately. Right now."

Outside, I said to myself that I had to think of an answer. Got to think of an answer when Father asks, *Where are you coming from? Where have you been? Why are you late?* Got to tell him about volcanoes, long division, and Christopher Columbus discovering America while sailing on the *Niña, Pinta,* and the *Santa María.* Got to tell him the principal needed help making posters for the class for the entire school and she picked me because I had the best handwriting. Posters of class rules like "don't run," "don't talk back," important rules. Twenty posters in all because the whole school needed posters in the classrooms and Mr. Albert asked me to write out the rules because I had the best handwriting. He'll like that.

Walk faster. Legs, go faster because it takes time to wash the rice five times or six sometimes until the cloudiness in the water goes away. Two, not three cups of rice. Wash the grains gently so they don't crack and break in half. Wipe the bottom of the pot dry or the rice maker will explode. Don't forget to push the button or else hard rice cakes will end up in the trash.

He's already had two drinks by now.

One more and he'll rub me to make my pretend tummyache go away. That's what happens after his third drink. He makes me pretend a tummyache so he can kneel at the side of my bed and stroke it with his big dry hand. When he says I ate too much or that the bean sprouts didn't taste right or that the apple had a worm in it, I know it's time to get into bed with only my underwear on so he can rub my tummy easily until it's feeling well again. He feels all right about touching my tummy when he thinks he's making the hurt go away. I keep my eyes closed and pretend I'm asleep. Rubbing my tummy to make the ache go away, it's all right. I open my eyes sometimes, and he's got his eyes closed like he's praying. That's when I start feeling soft inside and want to pray with him about maybe seeing Mother and Min Joo again. But the pictures are always changing and I can't seem to see. I don't know what I feel when I feel him feel me. It's all right, I pray, as long as he doesn't rub down too low or bury his oily face in me. It doesn't matter. Fine. I feel fine until I smell the fire and metal from his day's worth of welding, even after his last stroke, after he's gotten up, walked away, and shut my door tight.

The mornings after, while we're putting on our shoes, he always asks if my tummyache is all gone. The first time he asked, I told him yes it was all gone. But he shook his head, tapped his finger on my chin, and said that it wasn't all gone. Not all of it. Now when he asks, I tell him my tummy's always aching.

I ran up the apartment steps breathless, unlocked and opened the door. There was a woman sitting on our coffee table with her legs crossed. She was wearing blue jeans with a tight-fitting T-shirt that said, *Virginia is for lovers.* Her hair was long and permed. Her eyebrows were thin. When she tapped her pink fingernails upon the table, I remembered where I had seen her before. She made that same *tap-tap* sound against the cash register in Arirang Market. Her sandaled foot shook to the beat of a song that was playing on our stereo. The table was already set for dinner. When the woman saw me, she hopped off the table, approached me, leaned over, and extending her hand at me, she said, "Hi, I'm Loo Lah."

5

"How do you do?" I said, bowing at the waist.

"Fine, I'm just fine," Loo Lah said. She picked up her drink and walked over to my father in the kitchen, who was running the faucet over something in the sink. She held onto my father's arm and whispered in his ear. Two shopping bags from Arirang Market were on the counter. On the floor leaning against the refrigerator was an unopened sack of rice. With Loo Lah clinging onto his arm, my father turned the faucet off, dried his hands, and walked out of the kitchen toward me. Wearing the kind of stupid smile Boris wore on his face after a long kiss, my father told me Loo Lah-sister would prepare dinner tonight. As he walked into the bathroom, he told me to be helpful and thankful because Loo Lah-sister had brought us the food.

"Thanks for the food," I said, put down my school bag on the couch, pulled out my spelling book, and began memorizing words. Loo Lah asked what kind of a story I was reading.

"I'm not reading a story," I said. "It's a spelling book."

"Are you a good speller?" she asked.

"Quite good," I said, putting the book away and walking past her into the kitchen. I looked in the sink and asked, "What is this?"

"I'm making fish stew tonight," Loo Lah said, and ran water over the two fish. Tossing her hair back, she said cooking was a hobby of hers. She loved it. "I'm good at it, you know," she added. When I didn't respond, she asked me where the knives were.

Pointing to the top drawer, I said, "There."

As she cleaned the fish in the sink, she looked over her shoulder and said, "Ahn Joo, I wonder. I wonder if I were your age . . . How old are you?"

"Ten. Almost eleven."

"I wonder if I were ten years old again, and you were still ten, of course, I wonder if we would be friends. Or, I wonder if you were twenty-five and I was twenty-five, we would still be friends. I wonder how you would look at twenty-five. But I've always wanted a little sister. What about you? Did you ever dream of having a big sister?"

Shrugging my shoulders, I told her she shouldn't clean the fish in the sink because my mother never got the garbage disposal fixed because my little brother cried at the sound of it and also because a chopstick fell through and jammed it. My mother always bought her fish cleaned, and if the market was too crowded, she always cleaned her fish on the counter and threw out the unusable parts twisty-tied in a plastic bag in the garbage. Loo Lah probably brought home leftover fish from the market, fish that wouldn't sell. My mother always bought fresh fish. She always wore an apron when she was cooking. And her hair was never worn down, messy, falling in her face and falling into the food like Loo Lah's.

"Why don't you wash up and help," Loo Lah said. She tilted her head back and shook her hair away from her face.

"Your hair," I said.

"What?" She turned off the running water. Looking down at me, she again asked, "What?"

"I said, 'Your hair.' "

"What about my hair?" she asked, running the water again.

"It's falling into the food," I said clearly and loudly.

As she pulled out the guts of the fish, she told me to go get her a barrette or rubber band for her hair instead of just standing there and watching her like some dumb tourist.

"My hair's too short for barrettes. I don't wear them," I said.

"Then get me a rubber band," she said.

"They're in that drawer."

"Would you get one out? Can't you see my hands are busy?"

"They're too little to hold your hair," I said, walking out of the kitchen.

Loo Lah turned off the running water and in a teacher's voice told me to stop. I turned my head and saw one of her wet, fish-scaled hands fisted on her hip and the other pointed at me. With lips that moved in front of unmoving teeth, she said, "Get the damn rubber band and tie my hair."

"I have to put my books away. I have to get washed up," I said, and walked on.

In my bedroom, I sat on Min Joo's bed and recited the Pledge of Allegiance to keep from crying. I tried to keep my eyes open wide and fixed a stare on the latch-hook rug of three cats in a basket hanging on the closet door. I made that for Min Joo because he was afraid of cats. But as I heard my father finishing his shower and Loo Lah opening and closing the cabinet doors, my eyes began to brim over with tears. I wrapped my fingers around my throat and held my breath, calling myself the names I had called my brother for crying like a baby, but this reminded me of Min Joo and my mother even more. I closed my eyes and wished Loo Lah would disappear. But from the kitchen she called, "Ahn Joo! Ahn Joo!" And when I didn't immediately answer her, my father yelled from the shower, "Ahn Joo-yah, Loo Lah-sister is calling you. Answer her!"

On the closet doorknob hung my orange sweater. I tied it around my waist and left my room. I walked into my father in the hall. He had a white towel around his waist and a blue one covering his shoulders. A fine-toothed comb had smoothed back his hair. He smelled the way he did on Fridays, when he came home with enough money to take my mother, Min Joo, and me to a restaurant for grape sodas, hamburgers, and french fries.

I stopped him and asked, "May I go to Boris's? I have math homework, and I left my book in school."

As he brushed past me to enter his room, he told me to set my mind straight because in this country without a mind set straight, I would never be able to win first place. Loo Lah's see-through white blouse was hanging on my chair. She was cubing bean curd in her T-shirt, which was way too small for her. She had plump white shoulders, and the pendant of her necklace was tucked into her cleavage. I asked her where she learned how to cook fish stew. She told me her mother, who was living on Cheju Island, used to be a diver and sold whatever she caught that morning at her own market stand. Oysters twice the size of her fist; clams, seaworms, conch. "She's the one who taught me how to cook fish," she said.

"Where is she now?" I asked.

"Still on the island, but she stopped diving because she was losing her hearing."

"What does she do?"

"She works in a tangerine orchard."

I told her I loved tangerines, and leaning against the refrigerator, I told her the lightbulbs in my bedroom had burned out, and my father wanted her to give me two dollars to walk over to Pershing Market to buy new ones. I also wanted to tell her to turn the fan on and open the window because the neighbor didn't like the smell of Korean food and the steam from the stove could set off the fire detector. I stopped myself.

"Doesn't your father have any cash?" she asked.

"But he just got out of the shower," I said.

"Then wait for him," she said, and slid the cubes into the pot of boiling water.

"It's only two dollars. You'll get it back."

Pulling out three dollars from the back pocket of her jeans, she told me I had better be nice to her. "I need a new toothbrush. Mine is old. Could you do that for me?"

"What color do you want?"

"Blue, yellow, red, green, I don't care," she said, and stirred her stew.

I thanked her, put on my shoes, and left. The hall of the apartment building was beginning to smell like fish and rotten beans. I ran down the stairs, pushed open the door, and skipped around Burning Rock Court two times playing duck-duck-goose with the parked cars. My father's white Ford Fairlane was parked in front of Boris's apartment building. I tried all four doors and found the last one on the driver's side unlocked. I sat behind the steering wheel and pretended to turn on the ignition. I pumped the brakes, turned the front wheels, bounced on my father's seat, and imagined myself driving up and down the Rocky Mountains from New Mexico to Alaska and back to New Mexico again, where Boris with two real legs was waiting for me on our magic tree with grape-flavored Popsicles growing on the branches. My mother's cushion. Her cup holder and scented Christmas tree. Her eight-track tape of Lee Mi Ja, the Korean singer with large horse teeth, who sang sad love songs about crying in the pouring rain standing outside her lover's locked door. *Won't you let me in? Won't you let me in?* My father's ashtray was overfilled with crushed cigarette butts. My mother would have emptied it each week, tapping it on the pavement, instead of adding a half-smoked cigarette stained with lipstick to the heap.

When I saw the figure of Boris's mother in the lighted window, I ran outside, calling, "Boris, Boris!" Shielding her eyes, she came close to the window chewing food. When she saw me waving my arms, she opened the window and, puckering her lips, asked, "What is it, dear?"

"I need to show Boris something. It won't take long."

She turned her head, shouted something in Portuguese, and looked down at me, leaning her elbows on the windowsill.

"Boris is coming. What is it you have?" she asked, looking up at the sky. Boris's mother was out of her uniform and wearing a light blue robe, which made her look like an ordinary grandmother.

"It's a new bug for our collection. We have seven now."

"What're you doing outside in the dark like that looking for bugs?"

"I'm not looking for them. I just walked into it. My father wanted me to get his money from the car. See?" I held up the three dollars.

She turned her head, again said something in Portuguese, then, looking down at me, said that Boris was getting dressed because he had just taken a bath and we'd better not do anything that got us dirty.

Boris limped out the door of the building wearing a pair of jeans and a pajama top. His wet hair was matted down on his head, making it look like a soft potato. I wanted to hug him and smell the soap still in his ear and tell him I was sorry for kicking him and calling him retarded earlier in the day. Boris's mother pointed her finger at the moon and told her son not to be long because it was late, the time wolves hunted children. I told Boris to close his eyes. Taking him by the arm, I pulled him toward my father's car.

"Come on," I said.

"Where're we going?" he asked with his eyes shut tight.

"Almost there," I said, opening the driver's door to my father's car. I got in first and crawled to my mother's side. "Get in. Open your eyes. Get in. Sit down. Touch the wheel. See, turn it like this. Close the door."

I told Boris to pump the brakes, pump the brakes fast and hard. With both hands pressed firmly on his knee, he pushed down on the brakes, biting down his lower lip. When he pumped faster and faster, he grunted, then laughed out loud, showing me his gums and teeth.

"Isn't it fun?" I said, and sat the way my mother sat on Friday afternoons, when she was at peace with my father. Her arm was planted on the armrest between the two of them. Her legs were folded and tucked as if she was sitting on a floor; they were neatly covered by her skirt. Her slanted torso leaned toward my father, who never noticed any of it at all. I pressed down my shoulders, let my hand casually hang from the edge of the armrest, and sat close to Boris like a loving wife and mother.

He put his right arm behind me, gripping my headrest, while the other hand held the wheel. Looking over his shoulder, he turned to check if the road was clear, then proceeded to back out of our driveway. He was a good driver, a good man, a good husband and father.

"Boris, I love you," I said.

I lifted the armrest, pushed it back, rested my head

on his thigh, and told him to pet my cheek. He petted my cheek and said he wanted to kiss me, and as I was telling him I didn't want to sit up yet, I noticed the corner of a glossy, colorful picture sticking out from underneath my father's seat. Reaching between Boris's legs, I pulled it out halfway. An American woman with beautiful long hair had a finger between her parted lips. Her eyes were closed, her neck stretched out long, and there was a gentle breeze blowing her hair away from her face. As I pulled the whole picture out, I saw her shoulders and breasts, then her other hand, which was touching the private triangle between her opened legs. I quickly sat up and showed it to Boris, who placed it on his lap and stared. There were more pictures of naked women, colorful, neatly cut out and unwrinkled, underneath my father's car seat. This was the hiding place for his most important things. As Boris and I handled the pictures, we kept them low on our laps so no one would see. The lighted windows seemed like eyes to me, and I sank deeper into my seat. Boris and I said nothing to each other. My stomach was full of hungry bugs, and the pictures made me want to go to the bathroom.

I had never known these women were in the car with the four of us when we rode to the New Covenant Korean Church, to the dentist's office, to cabbage farms and radish fields, to restaurants and liquor stores. . . .

Boris's mother called out from the window, and we looked up quickly. The pictures slid out of his hands to the floor, and Boris left the car without saying good night to me. As I watched him limp back to his mother, I was certain he would never ask to kiss me again. I piled the pictures neatly one on top of the other, hid them under my father's seat, and crawled to his side to let myself out. Then I walked into our building, sat down on the first step, and waited for my father to come out and call my name the way Boris's mother did.

Two moths were drawn to the hall's light. One landed on the glass case and the other fluttered in circles. The sound of television music and children came from apartment A. There was also the smell of Salisbury steaks with gravy, carrots and peas, a glass of cold soda, and for dessert a slice of chocolate cake. I imagined there would be a baby behind the door being gently bounced to sleep on a mother's hip, a rocking chair, opened coloring books scattered on the rug with uncapped Magic Markers and broken crayons.

I was hungry for Loo Lah's fish stew. Sucking the top button of my dress, I climbed the steps to our apartment and opened the door. The wraparound strings of her blue canvas sandals had fallen over, around, and underneath my father's boots. I picked his boots up, shook off the dried dirt, tucked the laces, and placed them against the wall.

On the dining table were two rice bowls, one empty and the other with two spoonfuls of rice left over. A pair of wooden chopsticks was balanced on the bowl's rim. In the center was an unfinished pot of fish stew. I tilted it and found the head, fin, pieces of gray skin soaking in jelling orange liquid; chopped green onions, cubed bean curd, and dried red pepper flakes. On the corner of the table between the two rice bowls lay a pile of fish bones on a page torn out of the telephone book. My father and Loo Lah had sucked on the bones and spat them out together. There were plastic containers of side dishes: lotus roots in sugared soy sauce, fried and salted kelp chips, pickled perilla leaves, pickled fish guts, pickled dried radishes. The plastic lids were neatly stacked on the other end of the table. The labels read: *$1.49 Arirang Market. $.55 Arirang Market. $1.15 Arirang Market. $2.39 Arirang Market. $.98 Arirang Market.*

Heavy breathing came from my father's bedroom. His door had not been shut tight. I peeped through the crack. The blinds were pulled up. The moon nestled in the window's upper-left corner. The calendar was still in the month of May. My eyes moved toward the left of the dresser, half its mirror cut off by the frame of the door. I saw only half of Loo Lah's wave of a bare back growing out of the dresser top, her calf pasted to the back of her thigh. She sat like a frog about to jump off one lily pad onto another. I saw half of her permed head, which my father's hand seemed to clutch and sway. One of his legs hung over the dresser. His foot rested inside an opened drawer. The metal handles clinked.

I returned to the dining table. There were four fried kelp chips left over. The rice was drying in the bowls. They would be hard to wash later. I carried the two to the sink. After rinsing them in hot water, I returned to the table, sat in my father's seat, and with one hand rattled the kelp chips in their plastic container and with the other traced the printed thank you on its label. I thought. I thought hard, and quietly told myself all this has got to change.

6

I hated Tuesdays because Boris had to go to Mrs. Chambers's office during recess to recite over and over again something about a Peter Piper picking pecks of pickled peppers. After he finished telling her about Peter, he had to tell her about a Sally on the seashore with seashells, while I was left alone with no one to play with.

I curled my fingers around the wire fence and shook it. It sounded like the noise I had heard monkeys make in their cages when our class visited the National Zoo. I had stared and stared at the mother monkey with her baby clinging to her back, wondering if she would ever hang upside down on a branch to get it off her back. I had decided their asses were red from all the spanking. I let go of the fence and walked toward the baseball field, where Max and Roger and Mark and Lucas and Linroy and Tyrone and a whole bunch of the boys from our class were chasing each other, trying to touch an arm or shoulder or neck or back before anyone made it to the end zone. I stopped, dug the right toe of my shoe into the grass, and thought about Boris sitting close to Mrs. Chambers, who had long blond hair, long legs, and long eyelashes that curled up to the heavens. Her knees would touch his. They would make funny shapes with their lips and catch each other's spit. She would lean close to Boris and tell him to place the tip of his tongue on the edge of his teeth and say, "Thermometer." I wanted Mrs. Chambers to disappear in her cool, dimly lit office, where the blue venetian blinds were always pulled down low, so that on Tuesdays during recess I would be the one to seesaw with Boris again and listen to his stories about Peter and Sally.

On the seesaw, Torpedo Tits Tammy was laughing while holding poor Ruthie up in the air. It wouldn't be too long until Tammy got off and Ruthie came crashing down. The Chinese girls played Chinese jump rope, chanting the days of the week in Chinese. I tried to join them once, but they told me they were already an even four, and it was impossible to play with a fifth. The black girls double-dutched to *ma name ma name ma name ma name is Jolisa Jolisa ma boy ma boy ma boy ma boy is Lalarnie Lalarnie.* After they sang their names and their boyfriends' names, they broke into a chant about eating sardines with pork and beans. Eddie and Mitchell swung on the monkey bars all recess, trying to get blisters the size of silver dollars on their hands so they could show off and make money from the stupidheads who would pay a dime to touch the bubbles and a quarter from the dum-dums who wanted to pop them. Next to the monkey bars were the tetherball people, and next to them the four-square people, and the hopscotch people and the relay-race people, and the people who swung on swings and slid down slides.

I watched them all and continued to dig the toe of my shoe deeper into the grass. When I saw that my shoe was turning green, I wiped the leather with my sweaty hand, walked back toward the school, and sat against the brick wall where Sun Joo, the new Korean girl, read her Korean comic books. When she first walked into our class two weeks ago, she was wearing the same white blouse, dark blue pleated skirt, and pink sneakers labeled "Star Runner," and I was embarrassed to have been born in the same country. She had large teeth, which made her mouth stick out like a horse, and she smelled of soy sauce and fermented beans. When Mr. Albert told me to sit next to her and talk in Korean because she hardly spoke any English, I told him I was unable to help because I had forgotten all my Korean words. Sun Joo, Ahn Joo. We shared the same middle name, and the others asked if we were from the same family. When I told them my name was Ahn Joo, and she was a Moon Gentile, the smart ones understood my joke and laughed.

In Korean I asked, "What're you reading?"

She looked up, startled. As she pushed her glasses back, she leaned against the brick wall and said, "Oh, so you do know how to speak Korean. And all along I had you for a dumb immigrant. How many years have you lived in America?"

"Long enough to know that those are ugly sneakers you have on," I said.

As she gathered her comic books in her arms, she called me a deaf-mute and told me to go follow my American classmates around. She stood up, walked to the flagpole, sat near the daisies, opened her book on her lap, and laughed out loud. I wanted to stuff her open mouth with clumps of grass. I pulled some out and threw them in her direction.

From around the corner of the building, I could hear

the voice of Stephanie Fenno. She was telling Lisa, Debbie, and Melanie a really funny story.

"Listen. Listen. There was this girl named Matilda. She was really fat. I mean *really* fat, and she was walking home from school. But these three boys, they were standing next to the flagpole, and they called her over. They said, 'Hey Matti, come over here. We want to ask you something.' Matilda went over to them because she thought one of the boys was cute. He told her he'd give her a quarter if she climbed the pole. So she climbed it halfway and shouted, 'Is this high enough?' And the boys said, 'No, go higher. To the top.' So she climbed to the top and got her quarter.

"This happened for three days, and each time more boys came to watch Matilda climb the pole. When she went home and showed her mom the quarters, her mom got angry and told her to stop because the boys were only doing that to see her underwear.

"But the next day, when the boys told her to climb the pole again, she climbed it anyway. She showed the quarter to her mother, and her mother slapped her. 'I told you they only want to see your underwear!' Then stupid Matilda said, 'But Mom, I wasn't wearing any this time.' "

The girls broke into roars of laughter, and I imagined Debbie poking her elbow into Stephanie's side and Lisa covering her pretty mouth with her pretty hand. I crawled into a cool shade so that the girls' laughter sounded far away and Sun Joo could not see me. I pressed my knees together, wondering how the pole must have felt between Matilda's legs. I slowly squeezed my forearm between my thighs and pulled it up close to my crotch. Matilda wasn't so stupid. She knew what she was doing. I pressed my forearm harder against myself, but once I started to feel something down there, the bell rang.

"Ahn Joo, didn't you hear me? I was calling you," Boris shouted, looking up at me.

"Nope."

"I called you pretty loud," he said, but I didn't answer him. Boris placed his hand on the twelve-foot pole in the center of Burning Rock Court. Trying to shake it, he called out, "Ahn Joo, what are you doing up there?"

"Can't you see for yourself? I'm hanging," I shouted back.

"What are you hanging there for?"

"Because it feels good. This is how you make yourself go to the bathroom. I'm busy, Boris, so why don't you just go home and do whatever you do?"

"Don't you want to come over and play?"

"Boris, you don't have a leg, and two people can't hang together on one pole."

As I watched Boris walk to his apartment, I told the pole that Boris was stupid to have a crush on Mrs. Chambers just because she listened to handicapped boys say tongue twisters all afternoon. She was married, too old for him, and probably had children our age. What did they talk about today? Old MacDonald moving mountains on Mondays?

I clung to the pole, smelled the metal, and picked at the rust with my thumbnail. Mr. Albert, Miss

Martin, the librarian, the secretary, Mrs. Lubbock, the guidance counselor; they were all so damn nosy. What's it to them if I throw up my breakfast eggs all over their desk while I hand them my lunch money? What's it to them if I wear the same jumper every day of the week? What's it to them if my father can't meet them for conference time? I wish they'd stop asking me about my mother. How many times do I have to tell them that she's on vacation and can't chaperone those stupid field trips to the Kennedy Center, where everyone has to bring a bag lunch. How was I supposed to know that once I opened the foil, the *kimbop* would stink and leave seaweed pieces in my teeth?

I remember how my second-grade teacher stooped down and blinked her eyes when she asked me about brushing my teeth. Ann, have you been brushing your teeth? Do you know what I mean? She made a fist and shook it left and right next to her exposed teeth. And I smiled at her while answering in my head, No, Miss Martin, I don't know what you mean. We don't brush teeth in our country. We let them rot. See? I saw her. I saw how Miss Martin's eyes looked over at me when the lice inspector told her the entire class was clean except for one student. I saw how her eyes grew big with surprise when he whispered the description of the little black boy sitting at table four, instead of the Chinese girl at table six. I'm not Chinese. My father's not Chinese. My mother's not Chinese. Loo Lah's not even Chinese. She's my father's girlfriend.

My father wants her to be my new mother because the real one left. He found Loo Lah behind one of the cash registers in Arirang Market. She used to sell rice cakes, green and pink fish cakes, instant noodles, rock candy, and sacks of rice. Loo Lah used to bring my father and me food from the store. But once she came to live with us in our apartment, she quit her job at Arirang Market. Loo Lah now takes long hot baths, shortens and takes in the waist of the dresses my mother left behind, covers our beds with sheets—American style—listens to love songs, and watches television to improve her pronunciation, while my father welds silver fences around parking lots all morning and all afternoon. She cooks bean cakes, makes rice wine, pickles radishes, and makes rice with sweet corn, my father's favorite. He calls her Lah-yah. He tells me to call her Sister or Little Mother. But I can't.

I try not to call her at all. But when I find her hair, long and permed, all over the bathroom floor, I become angry and say, "Little Mother, clean up the bathroom floor or shave your damn head." She cannot mother me. Loo Lah's only twenty-five years old. Although she feeds me, she cannot press her lips together as she chews her gum. She falls asleep on our sofa to the noise of the television. After eyeing me, she suggests I condition my hair with hot oil, pierce my ears, pluck my brows, and if my father is willing to pay, have folds surgically formed on my eyelids. She croons popular Korean songs about how a lover could so easily leave her beloved with the excuse of teaching him the sadness of love or with a good-bye note tucked in a bouquet of chrysanthemums or a drawerful of unmailed love letters. When my father leaves us alone in the apartment, he hopes that on his return he'll find me sitting on the floor between her knees, while she brushes and braids my hair. But my hair is too short for braids. He hopes to find her frying bean cakes while I stand behind her stirring the batter. Instead, he finds a snoring Loo Lah lolling on our sofa.

All she knows how to do is bathe, shampoo, feed, and groom herself. Her nails are painted pale pink. Her brows are plucked and drawn in. Her face is massaged. She has the awful habit of picking at the mascara clumped on her eyelashes, which look to me like the legs of an ant. Loo Lah's not my mother. No matter what, she never will be. Loo Lah will have to pack her things and leave when my real mother and little brother return.

I remember when my father worked overtime all week and finally when Friday came around, he came home early, about four o'clock, with his paycheck. My mother turned off the stove, untied her apron, and went into her bedroom to change into her brown dress with the pink baby umbrellas on it. When she came out, her hair was long and wavy, and I could tell she had just brushed it. She was wearing red lipstick and blue eyeshadow. Min Joo and I put our shoes on and waited at the door, while our mother and father got ready. She walked from the radiator in the kitchen to the one in the living room, then to the one in our bedroom, looking for her pantyhose. The water in the bathroom was running, and we could hear our father humming. Min Joo and I, tired of waiting, played *Gahi Bahi Boh,* which the stupid kids at school called paper, rock, scissors. *Gahi Bahi Boh.* Min Joo held out a fist. I held out two fingers. Our mother and father came into the living room. Father was slapping his shaven cheeks, smiling and singing, *Hurry, let's go.*

Min Joo always sat behind Mother, and I always sat behind Father. Min Joo wanted to play *Gahi Bahi Boh* some more, but I told him no. Then he wanted to play *Mook Jji Bbah,* but I told him no. I simply wanted to sit still and watch Pershing Market, Buckingham Theater, Rosenthal, AOK TV move along outside while I listened to the Carpenters singing about rainy days and Mondays always getting them down. When Father whispered how much he made this week, Mother smiled, so I thought this would be a good time to tell her what Mina's mother had said about Min Joo and me. She said Min Joo had Mother's personality, but looked like Father. I had Father's personality, but looked like Mother. When I said that, my mother turned her head toward me and snapped, *So you really believe you look like your mother?* I sank into my seat and sang, *Hanging around, hanging, nothing to do but frown, rainy days and Mondays always get me down.*

When we got to the restaurant, Father ordered four Gino Giants, four medium french fries, four medium Cokes, and a small coleslaw for Mother because she had to have a side dish with her meal. Father wanted to sit at a table next to the men's room so that he could watch his Ford Fairlane from his seat, but Mother said the smell was making her lose her appetite. So Min Joo and I moved to another table, and I waited for her to give me my Gino Giant. She picked up the tray of food. Father lit a cigarette. She walked toward the table Min Joo and I had chosen. Mother's purse slid off her shoulders and landed on her forearm. The tray shook. One of the Gino Giants, which was still in its wrapping, fell to the floor. She picked it up, blew on it, and put it in front of me. That was the only time she ever served me first.

I was born first. The firstborn was supposed to get everything first. So why? Why did she always buy him new pants and shirts? Why did she feed him first? Why did he get the cotton quilts, while I slept with sheets? Why did he get a two-wheeler when he didn't even know how to ride? I knew the plums were hidden for him.

I remember when Min Joo broke the vase Grandmother sent from Korea. Mother had told him not to bounce balls in the living room, but he did. When she heard the vase crack, she rushed in, leaving the water running, and she yelled, *Ahn Joo-yah, go find the back scratcher!* I knew the stick was on her dresser, so I quickly fetched it for her. I said, *Here, Mother.* She looked at me and said, *That was awfully fast. So you want to see your brother beaten, huh?* And she pushed me against the closet doors.

Why did she give me the broken pancakes? Why did she thin my milk with water, not his? Why did Min Joo get to eat some of Joon's applesauce, not me? Why did she brush his hair and not mine? Mine was longer. Why did she take Min Joo with her, and not me?

I remember when I turned nine, my mother made me seaweed soup with mussels. I wanted to thank her by eating it all up while it was steaming hot, but I did not know the steel bowl would burn my fingers. I dropped the bowl, and the soup spilled all over my lap.

My mother struck me across my right ear and told me I was an ungrateful, clumsy daughter. That evening I saw her knitting in front of the television. I sat near my mother's feet, watched with her, waiting for the right moment to tell her how sorry I was for spilling her soup. We sat quietly for a while, until she jerked my shoulder back to take a look at my face. My mother saw me crying, and she pointed the knitting needles at my nose and asked, *What did I ever do to make you so miserable?* When I didn't answer, she yelled, *Ahn Joo-yah!*

My mother blamed me for burning her cooking. She blamed me for the broken fan, the crank calls, the cockroaches. She blamed me for Min Joo's crying. She blamed me for Father's drinking and Father's magazines. She said it was because of me we came to this awful country. Then my mother put down her knitting and cried herself, mumbling something about being a bad mother, killing herself or running away. I quickly wiped my face and told her I wasn't crying, that something got caught in my eyes, that I was all right, that I was sorry, and that I didn't want her to die or go away, *please.* But she poked her toe into the center of my chest and said it was too late.

My mother let Min Joo cry, but she never let me cry, so I hid in my closet, biting the edges of my blanket. She caught me once and yelled, *What are you crying for? Did your mother die? What are you crying for?* She pulled me out of the closet and told Min Joo to look for the back scratcher. Min Joo was glad he did not know where it was. He did not like listening to the stick *whoosh* through the air, then land *slap* on my skin. He did not like seeing those red rectangles on my calves. When Min Joo came back saying, *Mother, I don't know where it is,* she went frantic until she remembered using it in bed the night before to scratch the back of her head. She had left it under her bed.

Pointing the stick at me, my mother chanted, *What are you crying for? Did your mother die? What are you crying for?* The head of the stick landed on my arm. *What are you crying for? Did your father die? What are you crying . . .* Before she could finish, for I knew the slap would come right after, I yelled, *I'm crying because you like Min Joo more than you like me!* Taking a deep breath, my mother said, *So that's why you're crying. And you're not going to stop? Aren't you going to stop?* And the stick came down on my back. *You stupid, stupid girl. Ahn Joo-yah, think hard. Think hard about it.* Scratching her ankle with the stick, she walked out of my room.

My father's car was turning into the court, and Loo Lah was sitting on the passenger's side. I let go of the pole, slid down, picked up my school bag, and ran to our apartment. I threw my things onto the couch and went into the kitchen, where I washed our dinner and breakfast dishes and filled three bowls with the steaming white rice I had prepared in the morning. With my thighs aching and my palms smelling like rust, I set three spoons, three pairs of wooden chopsticks, and three cups on the table. I removed a pot of bean sprout soup from the refrigerator and put it on the stove. I turned on the heat. While waiting for the soup to boil, I filled our cups with ice cubes and water.

Sitting on the couch with my knees sealed together, I opened my spelling book on my lap. When I heard my father and Loo Lah climbing the stairs together, I formed the words with my mouth: Might. Sight. Flight.

7

I taught myself how to read palms in Mr. Greer's fifth-grade class, when I was assigned to write a book report on Pan, half man and half goat, the Greek god of woods and pastures, the protector of shepherds and farmers, from whom the word *"panic"* came. I was looking him up in the encyclopedia, and on the opposite page was a photograph of a yellow palm with black lines under the heading *"Features of the Hand in Palmistry."* Each line had a label: line of the heart, line of the head, line of marriage, line of fortune, line of health, line of life, line of fate. I memorized them all, told futures, fortunes, and tales during lunch and recess, and earned the name "Palmer" from the fifth-grade class of Sherwood Elementary.

The first palm I ever read belonged to Yvonne Weaver. She sat at table number four across from her boyfriend, Keith, who one day announced to the class that he saw his father suck on his mother's nipple in the hospital the day after she had delivered his baby brother. His father was black; his mother was Japanese. His baby brother looked Japanese, and Keith looked all black. Next to Keith sat Yvonne's best friend. Lisa had daddy-longleg legs, wore orange and green leg warmers in the winter, was the fastest runner at Sherwood Elementary. Sitting across from Lisa next to Yvonne was Judy. Judy drew horses on the margins of her math notebook, made origami swans with paper napkins, and had an older sister who was pregnant by accident. Whenever I walked by their table, I heard talk of love, animals, designer jeans, and nicknames, and I heard leftover laughter from one of Keith's funny stories.

When Yvonne laughed, her face reminded me of a Korean song my mother used to sing about a pretty face as pretty as a shiny apple and an ugly face as ugly as a pumpkin. Yvonne was the apple, and I was the pumpkin. She wore rainbow-colored beads in her corn-braids, and when she moved her head, they chinked against each other, the sound pearls made when being strung. Yvonne wore miniskirts and knee-hi stockings to match. She walked like a ballet dancer. Her skin was light, unlike most of the dark-skinned students in my class. She was class president, the captain of patrol, and won the Read-a-thon award for the most books read. And when Mr. Greer called on her to read aloud from *Our Western Civilization,* she had the prettiest lisp when saying her s-words. *Aphrodite is the goddess of love. She was born when she rose out of the sea. Her Roman name is Venus.* Everyone called her "Vonny," an animal's name, and I wanted to correct them, tell them that the "y" went in front of her name not after it, but I always plugged my ears, shook my head, and walked away.

On Yvonne's birthday, the class stayed inside for recess because Mr. and Mrs. Weaver brought us cupcakes, ice cream, streamers, and balloons for a party. Her father, a full-bearded dentist, had to duck in order to fit through the doorway. He hugged Yvonne, kissed her on the forehead, and pulled on her earlobe when wishing her a happy birthday. When she turned her back to him, he made rabbit ears behind her head and funny faces that made me laugh.

I wished I was Yvonne and my father was a full-bearded dentist. Yvonne's mother had freckles on her nose and wore tinted eyeglasses that made her look smart and important. She scooped ice cream into our paper bowls, telling us there was plenty for seconds. Yvonne decorated her mother with a necklace made of streamer links. I had once overheard my guidance counselor tell a parent over the telephone that the quality of the time spent with one's child was more important than the quantity of time together. Yvonne and her mother looked as if they had both quality and quantity time. While we sat in our seats with ice cream and cupcake, I looked over at Yvonne's mother and father, who were standing arm-in-arm near the doorway. They were watching their daughter at her seat receiving birthday wishes from her schoolmates.

"Happy birthday, Vonny."

"Happy birthday, Vonny."

"Happy birthday, Vonny."

As her parents left, Yvonne's mother kissed her on the eyes, and her father nudged her chin with his thumb. They shook hands with Mr. Greer, who looked like a little man next to them. He didn't look the way that he did on the first day of fifth grade, when he told us to "fear Mr. Greer." The three of them stood near the cake and ice cream table talking about Yvonne, and I wanted to hear. The two Chinese girls were at the blackboard playing a Chinese word game. Frank had chased Marcia into the closet behind the bulletin board. And the Iranian boys were chewing paper and throwing pencils down the radiator. I took my plate to the cupcake and ice cream table for more, and overheard Yvonne's father tell Mr. Greer that Yvonne was going to find a beagle in their front yard after school. As I was walking to my desk, Mr. Greer clapped his hands and announced that Vonny's parents were leaving and we should thank them for the treats. We waved good-bye and screamed our gratitude.

"This is for you," said Lisa, and handed Yvonne a bottle of lotion with strawberries pictured on the label. They hugged each other, and Yvonne opened the bottle, took a sniff, dipped her finger through the opening, and rubbed some on her hands. Keith gave her a pink card almost the size of my notebook. She thanked him, but did not open it in front of the rest of us. I watched Yvonne and her table of friends from my seat and decided I would read her palm.

"Yvonne, Happy Birthday," I said in a hoarse voice, standing behind her. She looked over her shoulder and thanked me. As she was about to turn around, I quickly added, "Don't you want to hear your birthday fortune? I know how to read palms."

Yvonne said she never had her palm read before and did not know what to do. I told her to hold still while I read her lines and give me her right hand because the left always lied. She turned her seat to face me, and I kneeled on the floor to read her palm. Her table mates gathered around us, and feeling her mounts, I began to tell Yvonne that her mount of Apollo was in constant motion, always moving, which meant she would be a dancer someday.

"Do you like to dance?" I asked, and she smiled and nodded.

Keith, who was watching us over Yvonne's shoulder, laughed and said, "Everyone knows Von likes to dance."

Tracing her line of the heart, I told her that more than anything else in the whole world, she loved animals.

"What kind?" asked Keith. I wanted to stand up, push his face away, and tell him: the kind with four legs and a tail, you don't qualify. But I stood up, let Yvonne's hand go, stepped back, and smiled. Those who had huddled around us asked, "What?"

"What is it?" asked Yvonne.

"Before the day is up—" I paused.

"What?"

"You're going to have a dog," I answered.

Keith said, "What kind?"

"The one I saw had short hair."

"Von asked for a dog last year, and she didn't get it," said Keith.

The others offered me their dirty palms, saying, "Read mine. Read mine," but I walked slowly back to my seat and drank the rest of my melted ice cream. Mr. Greer clapped his hands near the garbage can, singing, "Let's clean up, folks. Let's clean up."

When Yvonne saw me the next morning, she grabbed my shoulders, looked into my eyes, and demanded, "How did you know?"

"How did I know what?"

"My dog. How'd you know I'd get a dog?"

I told her my mother had the gift of telling fortunes, so did my grandmother, great-grandmother, and great-great grandmother. It was no surprise that the gift was passed onto me. When Yvonne thrust her open palm at me and told me to do it again, do it again, I saw her pretty apple face transform into a pumpkin.

"I don't give second readings," I said, and walked away. Yvonne stepped in front of me, her beads violently hitting against each other, and told me to come over to her house after school because she wanted me to do it again and to see her new dog. I told her I had piano lessons, to which she burst out, "Oh Ahn Joo, I play the piano, too! Then tomorrow. Come over tomorrow."

Up close, Yvonne smelled like the zoo, and I started to wonder if cornbraids could be shampooed, and if they could, did Yvonne ever shampoo hers? I told her I had piano lessons every day and walked into the closet, leaving her behind. I took longer than usual hanging up my sweater because I was feeling ashamed, guilty, and triumphant all at the same time.

When the rest of the class found out that Yvonne had received a dog for her birthday as I had foretold, they sat around me during lunch, and all throughout recess they followed me from the swings to the merry-go-round and back to the swings again, holding out their palms to me. I charged a quarter for a reading.

The girls lined up at the foot of the monkey bar waiting for their turn to be called up one by one. To one I would ask if she played a musical instrument, and if she did, I told her to keep at it because her ring of Venus, which represented love and music, was the strongest I had ever seen. To another I said she should stop spending so much money and start saving before she became a bag lady because her line of fortune, faint and weak, looked as if it would vanish by the time she turned twenty. There were too many gaps between her finger joints, which meant money easily slipped through—something my mother had said about me. To another whose nails were bitten down, I told her if she kept biting them, demons would enter her body, strike her mute, then infest her intestines with white tapeworms. To another whose hands looked just like mine, whose line of fate ran right through her line of head and heart, I stroked her cheek to comfort her and told her to keep a sharp eye on her mother lest she run away.

When Mr. Greer found out I was selling fortunes, he told me to put an end to it. He said getting money by lying was the same as stealing, an offense to my conscience, and I should stop before someone got hurt. I asked if he wanted his palm read as well. I told him I'd tell his fortune for free, and he hesitated before telling me he did not believe in such nonsense and should send me to the principal for tempting him. I told him it wasn't nonsense, that I was gifted as my mother, my grandmother, and my great-grandmother had been. My great-great-grandmother had told the fortunes of kings and queens in the royal court. Mr. Greer said this was not a royal court, and palm reading was an inappropriate school activity. So I arranged to meet the girls secretly in the bathroom, the boys in the back closet.

To the boys, I told fortunes of becoming a zookeeper who kidnapped children and fed them to the animals, eating dog soup to get rid of nightmares, and kissing a girl's private parts to grow hair on their chests. When Larry pulled down Julie's pants and tried to kiss her private parts, Mr. Greer pulled him up by his collar and said, "You can't treat girls like that. What's your problem, boy?" Larry screamed that I had told him it was the only way to get hair on his chest. The class laughed out loud. They might as well have been laughing at their own selves because they all believed my stories and came back to me with their lunch and milk money to hear more.

Yvonne and Keith were the only ones who did not follow me around like beggars with open palms. During lunch, when I saw them sitting alone at the far end of the cafeteria table sharing secrets and Yvonne's thermos of apple juice, and ignoring me and my beggars, I began loving her again and wanted to play with her new beagle and give her a second reading for free. As I watched them, Lisa sat close to me, holding her palm under my nose. "Here's a quarter, Palmer. What do you say?"

Taking the quarter and glancing down at her palm, I told Lisa that she would have a long life—maybe ninety-five years. She was going to have three husbands—an astronaut, a surgeon, and a pastor. She would have two daughters named Kelly and Katie. I saw a lot of money, and she was to stay away from beaches because I saw water, sun, and sand with blood, which was an awful sign. And there was a good chance she would get straight A's. Then, remembering Lisa had long legs, I told her her mount of Mars was extremely high, which meant she was very athletic.

Lisa said, "It's high, huh?"

"Very," I said.

"Are they cute?" she asked.

"Who?"

"My husbands."

"The astronaut is ugly. The surgeon is all right. The pastor is really good-looking," I said.

"What's a pastor?" she asked.

"A man of God," I said.

Lisa saw Yvonne sitting at the other end of the table, and with her palm open ran to tell her what Palmer had said. Palmer said this, Palmer said that. "Palmer said I was going to marry a good-looking man of God."

I saw Yvonne shrug her shoulders, throw away her lunch, and walk out of the cafeteria with her thermos hanging on her pinky. I decided to follow her.

"Yvonne, I'll give you another reading. You don't have to pay me," I said, walking quickly to catch up with her. She stopped, turned around, and with tears in her eyes and the beads on her braids hitting against her face, she pushed her open palm against my forehead, watched me fall back, then walked away.

When I walked home from school that afternoon, I had a headache thinking about poor Yvonne alone with Keith, alone with her beagle, alone with parents who should have belonged to a circus. I was thinking about what fortune I would have told her if she had not pushed me so hard. *Yvonne, your luck is changing. It's changing colors, red, blue, green, yellow. . . .* Why did she hit me? As I turned into our court, I plugged up my ears to keep myself from hearing voices. I wanted to pull out my eyes to keep myself from seeing pictures and cut out my tongue to keep myself from telling tales. I wanted to tell Mr. Greer that my mother, grandmother, and great-grandmother were not gifted in any way, and my great-great-grandmother farmed pickles in the springtime and milled rice in the winter.

When I came home, Loo Lah was sleeping on the couch and the stereo was playing a sad Korean love song, which made my eyes tear. I went into my room, removed my white box full of quarters from underneath Min Joo's bed, and sat with its weight heavy on my lap. How could I pay for each lie I told? How could I pay for each quarter I stole? I picked one up and said to myself that this one belonged to Jaime, who wanted to know if his dead grandfather went to heaven or hell. He had died from smoking too many cigarettes, and Jaime was once told that smokers went to hell. This one belonged to Scott, whom I told to eat a tablespoon of baking soda every morning because his breath stunk. This one belonged to the girl whose lines looked just like mine and whom I told to always always, no matter what, keep her mother in sight.

I carried my box to my desk, and for each quarter wrote down the name and story I had told, filling the back and front of a sheet of paper with words. I folded it into a small triangle and took it with me into the kitchen, where my mother kept candles underneath the sink. With my triangle, a book of matches, a steel bowl, and a candle in hand, I walked toward the sleeping Loo Lah and sat down on the floor in front of her. The woman on the stereo sang so sadly that I thought maybe she knew how I was feeling. I lit the candle and burned my triangle telling God I would never read palms again, praying that He would forgive me and change me, make me blind, deaf, and dumb.

As I watched my writing turn to ashes, I sighed in relief and let the wax melt and drip into the bowl. I brought the flame close to my face, then held it to Loo Lah's, when I felt her turn on her side. She was dreaming about something—about moving on, taking the next step, going on: First her distant cousin, then my father, then would follow another man she could use as a stepping stone to go on to bigger and better things. During the year she had lived with us, I had become thankful for the way she giggled to get out of trouble and put my father at ease moments before his temper blew. My mother and I never knew how to keep him from kicking things. Loo Lah had a way about her that made my father smile, even if she was telling him she had driven his car all the way to Baltimore and lost his muffler on the way home. Loo Lah's arm dangled off the couch. I took her hand and held it close to my cheek, whispering to her how sorry I was for hating her, how beautiful I thought she was, how I loved the way she carved little boats out of apples. I turned her hand onto my lips and kissed her palm.

I read Loo Lah's palm by candlelight. Her mount of Jupiter was fleshy, which meant she was full of pride and ambition. She had no line of marriage, but a deep and beautiful line of the heart. I wondered how many men had taken her in, and how many she had left. As I began to trace her line of life, she moaned and pulled her hand away because the flame burned too close. When she opened her eyes and saw me with fire in my hands, she quickly sat up, turned on the lamplight, and called me a little bitch for trying to burn her to death. I blew out my candle, and Loo Lah slapped me across the face. She said she didn't feel sorry for me anymore. She said she didn't feel safe here anymore.

8

The summer I turned twelve, Boris asked me to go with him. "Go with you where?" I asked. He said, "Nowhere, you dummy. Go with me like boyfriend/girlfriend go with me."

For three days, Boris and I went together. The first day, he gave me a necklace strung with pearly buttons taken from his mother's sweater. The second day, he called me at midnight to play a slow song for me over the telephone. The third day, he told me to close my eyes. He held my hand, walked me to the ABC Drug Store, and bought me a chocolate bar, lip gloss, and a bottle of shampoo that smelled like coconuts.

The fourth day, Boris's father drove his truck back to Burning Rock Court from somewhere in Texas. Boris showed me the photograph of his father's new house in Houston. Two large trees grew in the front yard. Boris's father's truck was parked in the driveway. The windows had curtains on them; the shutters were green. Boris told me his mother and father were packing to move the next day. I asked him if he wanted me to return his gifts. He told me he wanted me to keep them.

"I'm happy for you, Boris," I said.

Boris, his mother, and his father disappeared into the front of the truck. The truck then rolled out of Burning Rock Court, turned right on Wilson Boulevard, and disappeared as well.

When I later told my father that Boris had moved away to somewhere in Texas and I was having a heart attack, he called me a stupid head for loving a one-legged foreign boy. "It's just you and me now. We're a team," he said with a smile.

My father was trying hard to be happy. Ever since Loo Lah left with the American man, who had long hair, a van, no children, and would help improve her pronunciation of English, help get her R's and L's straight, my father changed. He woke up an hour earlier than usual, jogged around the court, did push-ups in front of the television, and tried to read my schoolbooks. He told me to smile more. He told me jokes with punch lines that confused me.

My father told me to cheer up because he had good news. Certain I would hear that Loo Lah had called and was coming back for good, I plugged my ears and told him I did not want to hear good news today. He stood up from the couch, held my head in the palm of his hand, tilted my neck back, and said that from now on, he would be working in the city near the Washington Monument.

"Next to the pencil top?" I asked.

"I'm right in front of it," he said and inhaled on his cigarette. "But, Joo-yah, I can't do it by myself. You have to help me."

My father had saved up some money from his welding job, but it wasn't enough to buy a grocery store on 16th Street the way Mr. Kim did last year, or an AOK TV repair shop like Mr. Chun's, which stood between a flower shop and a liquor store fifteen minutes away from where we lived, or a carry-out in Northeast

D.C. like the one Yong Bin's parents owned. Yong Bin's parents used to be poor farmers in the most rural village in Korea, and Yong Bin's three older sisters used to walk around the village wearing rags while Yong Bin played in the nude. They ate porridge and chewed on tree bark. If they were lucky, they got to feast on crickets, rats, and squirrels. It was also said that Yong Bin's grandmother prostituted herself to black G.I.'s, who were known to love large lips and strong, radish-shaped legs. His parents never finished elementary school, and my father said that he doubted if they even knew how to read and write. They may have had bad blood, a bad name, and not known how to read and write, but they certainly knew how to count—count by hundredths, thousandths, tenths of thousands—because they now lived in a big brick house in Annandale, Virginia, and Yong Bin's mother's teeth were made of gold.

Although my father did not have enough money to buy a store, he did have enough to buy a white vending truck with a crushed left headlight and windshield wipers that did not wipe. Hot dogs, half smokes—spicy or mild, donuts, pretzels—salted or unsalted, chips, sodas—regular or diet, candy bars, chewing gum, aspirin, King Edward cigars, and egg rolls only on Saturdays. Plastic containers of sauerkraut, chili, relish, and chopped onions, which made me think of Boris, which made me cry. Squeezable bottles for ketchup, mustard, hot sauce, and duck sauce only on Saturdays. My father had never been an ambitious man, but Loo Lah in one year had taught him how to make plans, how to set goals, how to aim high.

When Loo Lah used to turn up one corner of her lip and say to him indignantly, "You're not planning to live here forever, are you? You're not planning to weld forever, are you?" he would shake his head, and a look of concern would come over his face; then for hours he would sit twisting napkins into long strips, not saying a word. Loo Lah had told him he'd better plan to save some money, move out, move up, buy a house, stop drinking, take care of me, and keep her from moving on to bigger and better things.

But Loo Lah had left, and my father flashed me his I-am-such-an-unlucky-man smile, shrugged his shoulders, and told me it was all for the better because she was using too much of our hot water and electricity anyway. Minutes later, he was in the bathroom, running the faucet trying to hide the sound of his whimpering. I wanted to kick the door down, turn off the faucet, scream that he was wasting the water, scream that he was to blame for everything—"Why didn't you kick her out? Why didn't you kick her out before she could ever leave us? And what about my mother? What about my brother? Where'd you put them? Hand them over to me"—scream my hatred of him for loving Loo Lah, Lah-yah, whatever her name was, and letting her sleep on my mother's side of the bed.

Purchasing the vending truck was Loo Lah's idea. My father never would have done such a thing on his own. He was content as long as he could go to bed with two bowls of rice in his stomach and a pack of cigarettes on his nightstand without the sound of my mother nagging him about going to church, going out of her mind, going back to Korea. Unlike most of the Korean families I knew, he did not bring us to America in order to make a million dollars. He simply wanted to run away from his father, who used to beat his mother crazy until he kicked her out for being crazy, then he married a second and third time, and still would have smacked my father silly for talking back and running the family rice mill out of business.

"Joo-yah, I need your help," my father said. "You get good grades in handwriting, don't you? And you're good at spelling, aren't you?"

I told him I had the best handwriting and would have been the spelling bee champion last year if I hadn't confused "truth" with "trust." I told him the teacher asked me to write out the school rules on a large poster board to hang on the bulletin board in the fifth- and sixth-grade hall. The poster board didn't even have any lines drawn on it.

"That's perfect. That's perfect," he said, and took out red and black permanent Magic Markers from his back pocket. My father wanted me to make cardboard signs for his vending truck. *Yes, we're open. Sorry, we're closed.* A price list of all the items we would sell. He patted my head and repeated, "That's perfect, just perfect."

On the first Saturday that my father took me into Washington, D.C., in his vending truck, I sat underneath the window next to a box of hot dog buns with the top of my head touching the stainless-steel counter on which the exchange of food and money took place. That was the only spot where no one could see me and from which I could catch a glimpse of the pencil top from my father's sideview mirror. I hoped no one from my school decided to visit the city that day because they might recognize my writing on my father's signs.

The cherry blossoms were in full bloom, and their scent came into our truck mingling with the smell of deep-fried egg rolls and roasting hot dogs and half smokes. I heard people passing by and began to remember the afternoon my mother had dressed me up in a yellow jumper with a pineapple-shaped pocket on my chest and Min Joo in red overalls, walking us around Washington, D.C. My father had walked four feet ahead of us, leading the way from one memorial to another. When we walked past vending trucks, I would see Chinese and Vietnamese torsos framed by large windows, and small bags of potato chips and corn chips that hung from clothespins; and whenever I caught sight of someone my age, I walked away feeling ashamed for her.

"You like hot or mild?"

"One dollar. Two dollar."

"Yes sir."

"Yes ma'am."

"Thank you. Thank you."

"Have good day to you."

"Is the good weather, huh?"

"Oh sure, *bu-ti-pul, bu-ti-pul.*"

As I grew tired of counting and correcting my father's pronunciation errors, I closed my eyes and leaned against the hot dog buns, telling myself he was better off underground, masked by a dark helmet, and welding the ceilings and walls of the Clarendon subway station. Quarters and pennies fell from the counter, bounced off my ankle, and landed onto the floor. As my father stooped down to pick them up, I heard a woman's voice from outside complaining, "How do you expect me to eat this half smoke? Do you realize it's practically raw?" Not understanding what was being said, my father nodded and assured her that yes, yes, this half smoke, mild half smoke. The woman said she knew it was mild; the problem was, it was raw. Before my father could once again assure her that it was a half smoke and that it was indeed mild, and before she could say that it was raw, raw, raw, I pulled on my father's pants leg and in Korean told him to give the woman a burnt one because the one she got was undercooked. "Oh, *law,"* he said, and happily replaced her half smoke with another. After she left, he clicked the tong and tapped it against the counter, and from where I sat, he looked as if he would break into a nervous dance like a circus monkey. He sat on a box behind the driver's seat, rubbed his eyes, and rested his head against the shelf that held boxes of Now & Laters, chocolate bars, peanut butter cups, lollipops, chewing gum, Jolly Ranchers, Fireballs, Tootsie Rolls, cigars, and M&Ms.

Throwing a straw at me, he said, "Why don't you get out of there and help? It's not easy, you know." He massaged his ankle with his right hand, while the other searched for a cigarette.

Curling up against the buns, I told him I was tired because I was studying the night before, and when I got through, I only slept for three hours because I was having horrible nightmares.

"What does a little brat know about nightmares?"

The sun was shining outside, and all sorts of sounds came in through our van window. Strollers, feet on concrete, feet on grass, cars, and talk, talk, talk. I could even hear the sound of people's hands rising to shield their eyes from the sun, fingers pointing to a building in the sky or to the perfect tree for lunch in the shade and a family snapshot. The roaster hummed above me. My father opened a pack of gum, and selecting two pieces, he asked again what kind of nightmares little brats had.

I gave him my I-don't-know-and-I-don't-care shrug, closed my eyes, and tried to remember the first five sentences of my story that would win first place in the school's annual writing contest. This year the students were to write on either "My Family" or "What the Future Holds for Me." My story began:

> *When I lived in Korea, I used to climb the cypress tree that grew near the village well. From the highest branch, I could see the gate, the tiles on the roof of our house, and the enclosed veranda where my mother would be peeling and stringing whole persimmons to dry for the upcoming holiday. She wore a beautiful green* hanbok, *and her hair was braided in a tight bun held by a jade pin. The Thanksgiving holiday is one of the most important holidays in Korea, when all members of the family gather together to pay respect to their ancestors. My name is Ahn Joo Cho, and I was born in Korea.*

My teacher loved anything I wrote that was about Korea. She sighed and became teary-eyed when I showed her Korean dolls, ornaments of straw slippers, drums, long pipes, back scratchers, chopsticks, and even silk flowers that were made in Hong Kong.

A customer came to the window wanting two salted pretzels. He tapped his hands on the counter and sighed, *ooo-wah, ooo-wah,* between each four count. I did not stand and look out to see if he was a black man, but I was certain that he was. After he paid and left, my father opened a bag of popcorn, ate a handful, dropped a piece on me, ate some more, and dropped another piece on me.

"Stop it," I said and tried to kick him. He dodged me. Sitting on the box behind the driver's seat, he threw popcorn at me and told me to get up, get out, take a walk to the pencil top, and if the line wasn't too long, take the elevator all the way to the top because you could see everything from there.

"I'm tired," I said.

Throwing more popcorn at me, he asked what would make a little kid so tired all the time.

"Not all the time. I'm just tired right now," I said, shaking the popcorn out of my hair.

"Aren't you hungry?" he asked, putting popcorn in his mouth. When I didn't answer, he extended his legs and nudged me with his foot. "Joo-yah, Joo-yah, aren't you hungry? Aren't you hungry?"

I sat up, pushed my back against the wall, pumped my legs and kicked my feet at him, breathing out I-hate-yous and telling him to take that, take that, take that. My father stood up, hopped around the truck like a boxer dodging my feet, and said, "You want to fight, you want to fight, huh?" Each time he knuckled me on my head.

"Stop it," I yelled, and tried to punch his knees, but he moved too quickly for me.

"Does that hurt? Does that hurt?" he said, knuckling my head harder each time.

"No, it doesn't hurt!" I yelled back.

"That doesn't hurt, huh? Does that hurt? Does that hurt?" he cried, pinching my arms and chest.

Trying to hold back my tears because I did not want my father to see that he had hurt me, I flapped my arms at him like a propeller. He grabbed my wrists and said, "What's wrong with this little brat? Is she going into some kind of a seizure? Joo-yah, stop it. You're going to run us out of business."

Min Joo and my mother were the last things on my mind, but when I spat at my father and he looked as if about to strike me deaf, I quickly cried out, "What did you do with them? Where's Min Joo? Where's my mother?"

He wiped off my spit with the back of his hand, then squatted down to pick up the popcorn, telling me to get back into the corner before I ran him out of business.

I returned to my corner and curled up against the metal wall with my back to him. Tapping my fingertips against the truck, I told myself that it was good I did not cry in front of him because he would have said or done something to make me laugh, and laughing would have been the beginning of my liking him. My wrists, shoulders, and spots on my chest tingled with pain. I tapped my fingertips against the truck, whispered Boris Bulber's name, remembering the afternoons we kissed; I was teaching him long division.

Boris Bulber. Boris Bulber. After that kiss, I had told him he looked retarded with his fluttering eyelids, shaking lower lip, and hunched-over back. His elbows on his knees and his palms over his ears, he had swung his head left, right, left again, repeating, "I'm not, I'm not. I'm not retarded."

I had wanted to catch his swinging head and cradle it on my chest. I wanted to carry Boris on my back along the trolley tracks my father had once driven past on our way to Arlington Clinic for my measles and tetanus shots. I remembered how the tracks made a circle around treeless hills of overgrown grass, the dried yellow leaned into and over the green. Next to the track was a baseball field, and between them, a creek trickled through. I saw the six-inch wooden slabs laid evenly between packed gravel, iron railings fixed to the ground by rusty iron nails, and heard the brush of the grass when the wind blew. Boris would be heavy on my back, but I would carry him around the trolley track, and when we returned to the place we had begun, I would take him to the steepest hill, whisper, "Boris, look how high we've climbed," and gently press him into the grass. Legs first, back, shoulders; then, cradling his neck in my hand, I would settle his head on the ground. But that afternoon when he asked me for another kiss, I kicked his shin, told him to wake up, told him to take his plastic leg somewhere else because I didn't have time to fool around with a handicapped boy who didn't know his long division.

With my fingertip, I traced numbers on the wall of

my father's truck, divided forty-five into one hundred and five, then traced letters, words, phrases:

Ahn Joo was here. BB + AJC together forever.

Then I wrote the next five lines of my story that would win first place:

Korea is divided into two nations at the thirty-eighth parallel, and the nation of South Korea is known as the land of the morning calm. Its capital city is Seoul, but I was born in a village near Pusan. My parents, grandparents, and great-grandparents were born there as well. The village is called the One-Hundred-Year-Old Mountain and is known for its saltwater fish, anchovy, and herring.

"Joo-yah, get out of there. You'll get sick. Take a walk. Eat something," my father said. "At least sit up. Go sit up there. You can push the seat back." I told him I was fine. "Aren't you hungry? Do you want a hot dog?" I was hungry, so I told him I would take one with mustard. I sat up to eat the hot dog and asked my father, "What's herring?"

"What's the spelling?" he asked.

"H-E-R-R-I-N-G."

The *World Book* in school had told me Pusan was known for its saltwater fish, anchovy, and herring. It also told me that Korea was known for strong family ties. Families lived in small villages, worked on farms, and remained loyal to each other. The family was more important than the individual or the nation. Grandparents, parents, sons, unmarried daughters, the sons' wives and their children all lived happily together. To illustrate this, there was a photograph of a family of twelve or more members sitting on a porch eating supper. In the center of the photograph sat a girl my age, with hair cropped above her earlobes, listening to someone who had been cut out of the picture. Her sisters and brothers were looking in that direction as well. I think they were having anchovies and herring for dinner.

My father turned his left ear up as if listening for distant music, repeated the letters in order, and looked for his Korean-English dictionary in the front of the truck. As he fingered through the pocket dictionary, he asked himself what herring might be, what could it possibly mean? When he found the word, he pointed at it, and without lifting his eyes from the page, he said, "You're talking about *Chung uh.*"

"Herring," I said and stood up to get a drink.

"*Chung uh* is very expensive fish," he said. Pointing his fingers at his chest, he continued, "It's blue. It has very many tiny bones. You can eat them, the bones, that is. We caught some at . . . where was it? Was it in Woodbridge? Was it in Octon River? Acton? Octon? They're this thin. Remember we caught so many that we threw some away? But they weren't the real kind. They're good fried. They're called *Chung uh* because they're very blue, as blue as the ocean."

I told him I didn't remember fishing for herring.

"That's right. You didn't go," he said. He tucked the dictionary under his armpit and took my soda bottle to twist open the top. Dropping a straw through the opening, he returned the bottle to me.

"Isn't there a lot of herring in Pusan?" I asked.

"There's plenty of herring in Pusan. But Pusan's known for its belt fish," he said.

My mother had fried us belt fish once in America, but after finding white, pebblelike growths on them, she never bought or fried another.

"Are you sure it's belt fish?" I asked, not remembering the *World Book* ever telling me anything about belt fish in Pusan.

With outstretched arms, he said they grew as long as belts that could hold up the pants belonging to a fat man. Holding his middle finger up at me, he said that his sister used to cut the fish into pieces about this long. I laughed at my father because he did not know he was signaling his daughter to fuck herself. Encouraged by my laughter, he continued, "The meat grows in four long strips. She used to pull off the two outer strips for herself because of the bones on the sides. She gave me the two inner strips. She used to fry them until the silver turned gold."

"What turned gold?"

"The belt fish. The skin of the belt fish."

Through our window, above the moving heads of the people passing by our truck from left to right and right to left, I could see the lawn. The great big lawn, big enough for three men to stand in a triangle and throw an orange Frisbee to each other. Picnic blankets were spread and kept from flying away by the weight of iceboxes, sneakers, strollers, and grandmothers, who could not go very far. Someone was rolling down the hill in a sleeveless shirt, and I shuddered because the grass blades would nick his arms good and his mother would yell at him, while he was still dizzy in the head.

He would be dizzy for a very long time. Four girls jumped around in black trash bags, chasing each other and screaming when one came close to tagging them. Some people walked down the lawn. Others walked up the lawn to be closer to the pencil top, which was made of white rock and was standing tall above the moving flags and the seated people waiting to go inside.

"Where is she now?" I asked, watching a boy and a girl playing soccer with a basketball.

My father leaned back on his chair, stretched out his legs, and watched me finish my lunch. "You can have another," he said.

"I'm full," I said.

He sold a customer a Danish and two bottles of orange juice. Then he sat back down and told me that his sister was still in Korea. He called her *noo nah,* what Min Joo used to call me, and told me that she had once been accepted to study at one of the best women's universities in Korea, but the old man would not let her go, he would not pay for her tuition, he would not pay any of their tuitions, except the two youngest boys', who belonged to his third and favorite wife. My father said that when tuition day came around, he was quick to hide because the old man got angry. When the old man got angry, he was light with his heavy hand, quick to strike anyone. He didn't know how his brothers managed. They got their money, they kept off the farm doing minimal labor, they studied secretly; they loved studying, and they earned their medical degrees. My father told me that one of my uncles, the nose-throat-and-ear doctor, almost burned down the house while secretly reading by candlelight underneath a quilt.

But my father thought it was more important to get on the old man's good side by working on the farm. The old man would call him, *Shin-ah! Shin-ah!* My father mistakenly believed that working for the old man and his wife would somehow earn him some points—love points, he called them. But they called him only when they needed wood chopped, land plowed, water fetched. He would hear *Shin-ah! Shin-ah!* And he grew to hate the sound of his name.

But it wasn't my father who had it the worst in his family. Han-il *noo nah,* she was driven out of her mind and out of the house. After Grandmother was kicked out, my father said that Han-il *noo nah* lost it. She was wetting herself and listening with her ear pressed close to the walls. The old man's back wasn't strong enough to pull her away from the walls day in and day out, so he sent her away to marry one of his friends' sons. It was a business deal. He owed his friend some money, and this way he got his debt canceled. My father didn't see his sister for about a year. Then he got news that she was wetting herself and listening to the walls again. My father told me that she was now working at a Buddhist temple. She cooked the meals for the monks there. It was a beautiful temple, built on the side of a mountain, facing the sea. My father had visited there, a little outside Pusan. He said that Han-il *noo nah* seemed happy there.

For the rest of the afternoon I sat in the passenger's

seat, telling myself never to go to the *World Book* for stories, and thinking about my poor aunt Han-il and how she was terribly wronged by her family, my father included. Behind me came the sound of coins being dropped into the metal money box and my father trying to tell his customers to have a good day. I wanted to write a story about my aunt Han-il, giving her another life because I did not believe she could be happy cooking meals for a bunch of silent men. I refused to participate in her suffering; she would be redeemed from that life into another by my imagination. When my father visited his sister, he had not noticed the unhappiness in her eyes. He was betrayed by the beauty of the mountain, the sea, and the temple.

I turned around and asked, "Did she have children?"

"Who?" he asked, wiping off the counter.

"Your sister," I said.

"She had a son," he said, and explained that the father would not let her near the baby because he was convinced that her insanity was contagious.

That evening my father closed shop after selling the final egg roll. He tossed me a blueberry pie before starting the engine and said we would pick up cheeseburgers for dinner. As my father drove through the streets of D.C., he talked of having made this and this much money today, and if we kept this up a little longer, we would make this and this much by Christmas, and in no time we would have our own grocery store and live in a big brick house somewhere far away from Burning Rock Court.

"Do you like the sound of that?" he asked.

I told my father that yes, yes, it was all fine with me, but I was not listening to him. My mind had been on my aunt Han-il all afternoon, and during the drive back home she was still alive somewhere between my memory and imagination. I could not stop thinking about her and how I would save her from her misery. The sentences I had memorized and planned to write for the school contest were forgotten, and I began mouthing new words, new phrases, new sentences. As my father talked about good weather being good for business and bad weather being bad for business, I traced letters onto my left palm with my right index finger. I formed the first words of my new story that would surely win first place.

9

My teacher usually loved anything I wrote that was about Korea. But my submission for the Young Writers Contest disappointed her. She told me that the writing in my story about aunt Han-il was technically just fine, nearly professional. However, the story itself was difficult to believe. "One is required to suspend an unreasonable amount of one's disbelief," she said with a friendly frown.

Within three pages, I had written my aunt's life story. She was abused and driven to insanity by her father, stepmother, and brothers. Her father sold her into a marriage in order to have his debts canceled. Her husband tormented her emotionally, physically, and mentally. My aunt then ran away from her home to live in a Buddhist temple, where she cooked meals for the monks. Haunted by past memories, she returned to the family with poisoned rice cakes. Her father, stepmother, and brothers gladly ate them and died instantly. Aunt Han-il burned down the house, emigrated to America, worked as a secretary in a doctor's office, married a Ph.D., had two daughters, and lived happily ever after.

My teacher said that I had enough material for an entire novel, and I could not possibly do justice to my aunt's life in three pages. The ending was artificial and contrived. Returning my story to me, she asked, "Ahn Joo, do you ever hear voices?" Without giving me a chance to respond, she told me to listen to them.

When I laid down in the center of my room with my palms pressed on the floor and my eyes closed, I heard the voice of my mother. She told me to do this and do that, don't do this and don't do that, you're good enough for this, but not good enough for that. I memorized the way she sounded, so that when I woke up, I could go to my notebook and record it.

Third place went to a Japanese girl, who wrote a diary comparing and contrasting her life in Kyoto with her life in Arlington; second place went to a boy, who wrote about his blind father reading him and his little brother bedtime stories in the dark; runner-up was awarded to an essay called "How to Save the World Through Arts and Crafts," written by my classmate, Jennifer Beechum, whose father was a well-known painter of some sort; and I was awarded first place for my piece, "The Voice of My Mother."

My teacher returned it to me with a gold star on the top right corner of the first page. She said that it was a mature, honest, powerful, poignant, and sophisticated piece of writing, and I should give serious thought to becoming a writer some day. Jennifer Beechum and I were to read our writings during our graduation ceremony.

My father could not attend my graduation ceremony, which was held on a Wednesday in the middle of the afternoon, because he was working in Washington, D.C. When I showed him my report card for the final marking period and told him I had won first place for a story I had written about Mother, he asked, "What did you say? What did you say about her?" To put him at ease, I lied and told him I had written about the time she made me mussel soup for my birthday.

"I'm reading it tomorrow for graduation," I said.

Glancing at my report card, he poured more milk into my glass and said that graduating from elementary school was only the first step. Graduating from college, now that would be a real accomplishment. He looked at my report card again, pointed at all my A's, and told me I was his only hope.

"I hate milk," I said.

"Drink it or you'll stop growing," he said and put a spoonful of rice into his mouth.

That night I went to bed early because I could not hold back my tears. In bed I told myself to stop or else my eyes would swell and reading with swollen eyes was impossible. Clearing my throat, I practiced saying aloud: "My name is Ahn Joo Cho, and my essay is called 'The Voice of My Mother.' I have written something called 'The Voice of My Mother,' which I will be reading to you today. 'The Voice of My Mother,' a prose poem by Ahn Joo Cho . . . " And I reminded myself never to say thank you. Why should I, like a leper, beggar, orphan, thank them for listening to me?

When the principal called my name, Ahn Joo Cho, as the recipient of this year's Young Writers Award, I stood up and walked with bowed head to the podium where the microphone was waiting for me. Jennifer Beechum had already read her essay and she had received great applause that I did not think my reading would match. She had family in the audience, who clapped and yelped and blew sharp whistles her way. The auditorium was full. At the foot of the stage the school band was getting ready to play the closing song. My teachers were scattered throughout the room. The clock on the opposite wall read 12:30. I pulled down the microphone, cleared my throat, and in my most confident voice said, "This is 'The Voice of My Mother.' She passed away a year ago.

"Chew on parsley if your mouth tastes old. Smear chicken grease on your lips so no one will think you go hungry. Boiled dandelion leaves with sesame oil and seeds make you go to the bathroom. Raisins soaked in *soju* relax your muscles. Chew gum, it'll help you digest. But don't chew gum like that with your teeth showing. Just like those country cows. No one wants to see your crooked teeth. When you smile, keep your lips together. Don't scrunch up your nose and eyes like that when you laugh—you'll get wrinkles. Why do you laugh so loudly? What do you have to laugh about? What do you have to cry about? Did your mother die? Is that why you cry? Or are you crying because your mother's still alive? Are you going to stop the tears or not? Stop biting your nails. They'll think you go so hungry, you have to eat yourself. Who taught you to eat your fish like that? You leave all the good parts. Suck out the fish eyes, they'll make you see better. Don't make me buy you eyeglasses. Where do you go to buy eyeglasses here? Suck out the fish brain, it'll help you speak English. Then you can go buy your own eyeglasses. Chew on the bones, but don't swallow them. Chew and spit them out. America has no place to remove fish bones from a stupid girl's throat. Girls stupid enough to swallow fish bones deserve to choke. Don't hold your rice bowl in the palm of your hand. You want to make me a mother of a peasant? At home, eat slowly; outside, eat fast or everyone else will eat your seconds and thirds. But don't eat like you haven't been fed. Eat like a lady. Get your seconds and thirds, like a lady. But get your seconds and thirds. What do they feed you at school? Do you get enough? Crazy girl. Why aren't you eating? What are you going to live on? If you don't eat, you're going to be a midget. You'll never grow as tall as these American girls. Don't you want to look like them? Don't you want to be Miss America? Eat. Your hair won't grow. You won't ever need a bra. Your teeth will fall out. You'll stay ugly like that forever. Who's going to marry you? We'll have to send you back to the bridge where the lepers live. That's where we found you, underneath a bridge. You don't belong to me. No child of mine sucks on ice cubes used to freeze fish. Get away from me. You're so dirty. I can't believe you're sucking on those ice cubes. No one's going to marry you. Again? You're crying again? What do I have to do? You want butter and soy sauce in your rice? You want fried *kimchi?* You want fried anchovies, pork dumplings, kelp? Stop complaining. The cabbage here isn't the same. What do you want me to do, fly to Korea? How am I supposed to make you *shik keh* in this country? Even if I could, I wouldn't make it for a selfish, picky girl like you. You should know. You expect to find *jja jjang myun* here? *Been deh dduck, paht bing su, ho dduck*—in America? Eat what you have or starve. What do you want me to do? You want pink fish eggs, green fish cakes? You want rice cakes, don't you? You want dates and pine nuts? Where am I going to find rice cakes? Ahn Joo-yah, what are you crying for? Did your mother die? What are you crying for?"

There was an uncomfortable silence in the auditorium. When I looked up, I caught sight of my teacher, leaning against the kitchen door with her right hand over her heart. The two flute players below me yawned. There was a shuffling in the back where mothers began setting up trays of cookies, cakes, and donuts. When I said, "The end," the audience politely applauded. I reluctantly bowed, said thank you, and returned to my seat, where Jennifer Beechum, elbowing me, said, "Way too weird. Way too dark. Way too depressing."

That evening, my father brought home an electric typewriter that was missing its A and E keys and told me not to make any rice for tomorrow's dinner because he was going to take me to a Chinese restaurant. He asked how graduation ceremony went. Showing him my writing, proudly wearing its gold star, I told him I had read it aloud without making a single mistake, without stuttering once. He skimmed through the pages, palmed my head, tilted my neck back, and said that my writing was the prettiest he had ever seen.

10

When I told my father that a black boy on my bus was flicking cigarette ashes onto my head and telling me to bend over, he said he would drive me to my junior high school every morning. When I told him some girls laughed at my green jeans, my father said that he would buy me blue ones although green was a good color. When I told him my English teacher secretly drank Scotch out of her Dr. Pepper can and often fell asleep before finishing her sentences, and Miles the janitor was caught masturbating behind the trash bins during my lunch period, and the only thing my depressed algebra teacher ever talked about was his recent divorce, and some of the older students did not yet know the difference between a noun and a verb, a prepositional phrase and its object, the subject from the predicate, and I began bleeding, my father folded the *Korean Times* onto his lap and told me to pack, because we would be moving to Morning Glory Way in Potomac, Maryland.

On Halloween, my father enrolled me in my new school, called Weston Junior High, a five-minute walk from our new home. He walked me through the main entrance, dropped me off at the door of the main office, and reminded me to turn on the rice maker when I got home. Handing me a ten-dollar bill for lunch money, he asked if I had washed my hair in the morning because it looked oily. Looking at the other students passing in the hallway, he told me my blue jeans fit well on me and that I was a smart girl. I turned the knob of the door, said good-bye, and went inside.

When the school secretary asked what my father's employment was, I told her he was self-employed, a proprietor of some sort, had his own business here and there. When she asked what my mother did for a living, I told her she passed away when I was three years old from cancer.

"It's just my father and me," I said.

"Your counselor will be Mrs. Hubbel. She handles all the students whose last names begin with A through E. She'll have your schedule. Her office is right there," the secretary said, pointing my folder at the door with a paper jack-o'-lantern. "Once you see her, you'll be all set for your first day." I took my folder and waited outside Mrs. Hubbel's office. The paper jack-o'-lantern had sharp, jagged teeth, and dangling arms and legs made from black yarn. "Honey, you can go ahead and knock. Go ahead and knock," the secretary said, shaking her bangled wrist at me.

After my first two weeks of school, Mrs. Hubbel got it into her head that I was a troubled adolescent and made me meet with her daily for fifteen minutes to get to the bottom of all this. I had stolen a bottle of Giorgio perfume from the gym locker of a cheerleader, whose father was the president of Woodward & Lothrop. I had written pornographic love letters to Melissa Fintz, who ate her peanut butter and apple sandwiches alone in the cafeteria while reading useless teenage love stories. During gym, I had kicked the soccer ball into Jane Jordan's face when a game wasn't yet in session. I had cheated on my science quiz by sitting on my notes about cumulus clouds. I had torn off birthday balloons and streamers from someone's decorated locker. I had stolen books from the library.

Pitchforked veins grew from the pupils of Mrs. Hubbel's gray eyes.

She sat me next to her behind her desk. From her leather-upholstered, swiveling recliner, she leaned down at me and said, "If you want to succeed here and in your life, you must focus, concentrate, and apply yourself. My dear, you must apply yourself. I know adjusting to a new school is difficult, but you were not meant to be a delinquent." When I returned her advice with a blank stare, she grabbed my shoulders, shook me, and looking me straight in the eyes said, "Do you know how brilliant you are? Apply yourself."

She made me play games with her. Word association. When she said "blue," I said "sky." When she said "spider," I said "web." Black, night. Father, mother. Brother, sister. When I told Mrs. Hubbel to stop, she said, No, go.

When she asked how things were at home, I told her they were all right. When she asked what my favorite food was, I told her none in particular. The happiest moment in my life? I told her last Christmas was the happiest moment in my life. She asked why. I gave her my I-don't-know-and-I-don't-care shrug. Clearing her throat, she calmly told me to complete an I-feel sentence. I told her I felt fine.

I feel. I feel. I feel dumb like the rubber stiffs in

CPR class, except I have no one to pump my heart one-one thousand, two-one thousand, three-one thousand, four-one thousand times, then blow breath into me. I feel retarded and limbless like Boris Brace Boy Bulber, who now lives somewhere in Texas with his mother and father. I feel like breaking those curved wooden calligraphy pens into splinters and coloring South America black. I feel like telling Mrs. Hubbel that I know her games and tricks and that she'll never figure out why I'm failing all my subjects. She'll have no notes to scribble on her legal notepad and tuck away into the manila folder labeled "Cho, A. J. #127."

Stop asking me why I lied about my mother. I don't know where she disappeared to. I feel like stopping. I feel like stopping the bells from ringing every fifty minutes. I don't remember my locker combination. I can't run four times around the track within eight minutes. What do I do during flex time? I don't know where to go during flex time. There is no one to follow, no one to talk with, no one to ask where she bought her designer jeans and Docksiders. I feel like eating my lunch in the cafeteria at a table where my elbows can bump into other human elbows, rather than the metal graffiti walls of the toilet stall, and where I can hear conversations that don't come over the walls between flushes left and right of me. They won't let me sit in front of my locker and eat, they won't let me sit in the library and read, because it's our designated thirty-five minutes to take our afternoon meal.

I don't know the difference between integrals, derivatives, arc cosine, and sine for trigonometry. They put me in the wrong math class. I didn't ask to be put in a gifted and talented trigonometry, but they put me in anyway because I was quiet, looked Chinese, and wore glasses. I haven't even memorized my postulates and theorems for geometry, and doesn't geometry come before trigonometry? I don't have a baked potato for lab science. I won't dribble, run, jump, and throw the basketball through the hoop or underline the prepositional phrases, circle the prepositions, bracket the object of the preposition, and sing all the prepositions in alphabetical order to the tune of "Yankee Doodle Dandy": about, above, across, after, against, among, around, at, before, beside, between, beyond, by, down . . . What is the use? I want to read Jocasta's part, but I can't read it aloud without gasping for breath after every three words. But tell me, *gasp,* Oedipus, may I, *gasp,* not also know, *gasp,* what scares you, *gasp,* so? How am I supposed to give an oral report on how to use an abacus? I know how to use one, but how do I tell forty people?

I feel like rolling an iron ball down the hall to split the clusters of fours and sixes lingering near the lockers, talking amongst themselves about going to a movie Friday night—my mother will drive us, your father can pick us up, let's not ask her, she's such a nerd, did you know that Ellen and Chris kissed?

At nights in my new bed and my new room, I told myself that I was far superior to all of them. They were mere pigs living lives of mediocrity. There was no depth in their thinking; they were preoccupied with kiwi-flavored lip gloss, the hemline of their skirts, love notes folded into the shape of stars. They knew nothing of pain and suffering. To them, pain was not seeing their names typed on next year's cheerleader list. They drew red hearts on the margins of their world studies notes. They became embarrassed seeing their domestic help drag her flip-flops into the classroom with disheveled hair, smelling of disinfectant, a brown bag lunch in one hand, and a plastic bag holding a pink retainer in the other.

The students were simpletons who decorated other simpletons' lockers with streamers and balloons; all to ensure the returned favor on their own birthdays. And the teachers, who scribbled fractions of truths onto yellowing transparencies, leaned against overhead projectors that gave off more warmth than their own hearts.

I was not doing well in Weston Junior High, and I frantically searched through my father's dresser drawers because I wanted my mother.

Hidden in the tube of a brown sock were the three pictures of my mother:

GAP SOOL LEE

On the other side of this photograph, there was a date. It was taken on June 14, 1954. My mother was ten years old. She smiled, while her little brother pouted. That was how

Min Joo and I looked when we stood side by side. The last I heard, my uncle died of a heart attack. His ashes were tossed into a creek. I do not know what has happened to my mother. Sometimes I wish she has also died of a heart attack. I wish her ashes have already been scattered. Other times I wish she would come back and tell me how pretty my face has become.

For weeks I practiced holding my head in the same position, smiled so that dimples formed on my cheeks and my eyes took on the shape of the moon, wore a wide-collared white cotton blouse with a blue bandanna around my neck, and tried to live in a world that was black and white.

This is my mother with my best friend, Na-Ri. Our families went to the beach together. I wanted my mother to grab me and pull me into the picture, but Na-Ri was closer to her. Na-Ri's mother had a grocery store that sold instant noodles, cold red bean soup, fried dough stuffed with melted brown sugar, and piles and piles of notebooks stacked next to the front door, against the freezer, and on the shelves beside the cash register. Metal spiral notebooks, plastic spiral, lined, unlined. Pages as thick as rice paper; pages as thin as onion skin. Covers with drawings of blue birds, red shoes, elephant ears, and goldfish with puck-

SUNG HO KIM

ered mouths blowing bubbles that contained the American words, *I love you, Forget me not, Will you be mine?*

Na-Ri and I used to bang pots and pans in front of her mother's store and sing, *A monkey's butt is red, red is an apple, an apple is sweet, sweet is a banana, a banana is long, long is a train, train is fast, fast is an airplane, an airplane is high, high is the White-Peaked Mountain,* hoping to attract customers because if Na-Ri's mother made more than expected, she let us pick out anything from the store and take it home for free. Na Ri, squeezing her pack of chewing gum in her fist, and I with a new notebook tucked underneath my arm, kissed each other's ears before I walked through the back door of the store and home to my house.

I'm sure Na-Ri would remember me. I'm sure that when my mother and Min Joo moved back into the house, Na-Ri visited and asked for me.

Where is Ahn Joo?

She is studying in America. Min Joo and I had a more difficult time speaking the language. That is why we had to leave. We like it better here. But Ahn Joo wanted to stay.

But she will visit, won't she?

I wouldn't count on it.

What luck! She gets to study in America. She likes it there, doesn't she?

Very much.

Won't you miss her?

Very much.

When I am asked if I have any brothers or sisters, I tell them none. When I am asked where my mother is, I tell them she is dead. When I am asked how she passed away, depending on who my listener is, I tell them one of three stories:

If a teacher asks, I tell him she died of cancer.

If a friend asks, I tell him she got run over by a car.

If a stranger asks, I tell him she died giving birth to me.

11

Dear Mother,

This is to notify you of an address and phone number change. In case of an emergency, you may contact me at my new residence:

3309 Morning Glory Way
Potomac, Maryland 20854
(301) 555-2005

If you wish to contact Father's place of business, it is located at:

Good Food Carry-Out
100 South Capitol Street SE
Washington, D.C. 20001
(202) 555-0562

The home address and phone number were effective in the month of October, the place of business in the month of September. However, due to the excessive amount of energy and time required for the much-needed move, all notifications have been sent no earlier than today. . . .

Dear Mother,

Although it is highly unlikely that you would ever visit me, I am nevertheless writing in order to properly inform you that I no longer live in the apartment on Burning Rock

Court. It is a most fortunate move considering the neighborhood in Arlington, Virginia, was beginning to populate itself with the likes of criminals. There were a number of reported robberies, rapes, shootings. . . .

Dear Mother,

Father and I now live in a townhouse. It has four bedrooms, a living room, a family room, basement, a country kitchen, a garage, and two and a half bathrooms. We believe it is an excellent investment for our future. The quality of education offered in the public schools of Potomac, Maryland, far exceeds any education, public or private, in the Arlington area. I am already thinking about college. I want to study literature and write stories.

And what is in Father's future? A new van or truck for his restaurant.

Incidentally, the driving distance from Potomac to Washington, D.C., is considerably shorter than the distance between Arlington to . . .

Dear Mother,

Father does not know that I am writing you. But I feel, out of propriety, courtesy, and kindness, that I should write to inform you of our life which has changed beyond recognition. Father has changed beyond recognition. I have imagined about you and Min Joo's life in Pusan, I assume that is where you are, as I believe you have imagined about ours here. So that is why I write. . . .

Dear Mother,

Although I sit in our new home on a new chair with a new pen, listening to unfamiliar crickets through my new window, I cannot help but . . .

Dear Mother,

The window of my new room in our new home is open, and a silver moth has landed on the other side of my screen. There are mosquitos floating and waiting to be let inside closer to my lamp. Between my windowsill and screen, a groove holds dried flies turned on their backs and a ladybug covered with dust.

If it were daylight and I was sitting on top of my desk leaning forward, I could see the budding tips of the long, flexible ivy climbing toward me, the stack of chopped wood below. The weight of the wood with its rotting knots that house the worms, spiders, and red ants crushes the grass below.

But it is night, and all that I can see beyond the zigzag top of our wooden fence is a rich darkness, disturbed by a row of orange driveway lights with their hosts of spiraling insects. Beyond and above, there is the moon and the stars. . . .

Dear Mother,

I do not understand why you left me. Should I continue to wait?

Dear Mother,

As a young woman, I now see that you suffered greatly living with Father. You suffered greatly living with me. Your life here was torturous. You were unhappy, and what is greater or more rational than having as one's sole purpose in life the fulfillment of one's own personal happiness? And when you were given the opportunity to pursue a happier, more self-satisfying, comfortable and complacent existence without me, you did not hesitate. Your choice did not exactly heighten my hope for humanity nor was it one I would characterize as heroic, admirable, or meritorious. Your choice was that of any feeble-minded, well-fed, common woman. . . .

Dear Mother,

Father is not the same man, so if you have thoughts of returning, you are certainly welcomed here. . . .

Dear Mother,

Father has been telling me stories about Korea. My favorite is the one about the fox-girl and her brother. Do you know the story? It begins, "Long ago there lived a rich man who had a son but no daughter. He longed to have a daughter." The daughter grows up and kills her father's cattle by eating their livers. She kills the villagers and her parents by eating their livers as well. She then turns into a fox. It is a strange story, but one that is dear to me. . . .

Dear Mother,

One of the first and foremost concerns that should occupy all good mothers is whether or not her child is being well fed.

Our freezer is full of steaks. Our refrigerator is full of strawberries, carrots, and whole milk. Our cabinets are full of whole wheat, whole grain, raisin, almond, and date cereals. Our drawers are full of bags of dried black, Grand Northern, and kidney beans.

The above listing of foods is not necessarily a response to the addressed mother's concern since all concern is either the product of the addresser's imagination or nonexistent. The listing is actually an attempt to span the breach between what-is and what-ought-to-be. . . .

12

"Dad, you're going the wrong way."

"This is right way."

"Dad, you missed our turn. You had to turn at the light. You missed it."

"You push me. Stop pushing."

"Well, *you're* pushing me. I have to be home. I have work to do."

"That's why I take short way."

"Shortcut, Dad. It's called shortcut. Anyway, this isn't a shortcut. You were supposed to turn on New York Avenue. You just want to pass Angela's mom's store."

"Joo-yah, stop pushing!"

My father switched gears, pushed the accelerator, and made a sharp left turn onto a street that intersected with an old railroad track. Driving over it made his van bumpity bump bump and the box holding his hammer, pliers, electric drill in the back spill out, spread, and clatter. I opened my window, stuck out my arm, and could smell the liquor reeking from the clothes, breath, pores of the white-haired black man sleeping against the pitch-it can in front of *Fish Boat—Come In We're Open Fresh Seafood Every Day.* Fresh? There was nothing fresh about the barred-up windows and doors, stinking alleys used as urinals, purple plastic flowers pinned on the hat of a churchgoing woman with oceanic breasts, and these ugly brown vinyl seats smelling of spoiled ground beef fried in bacon grease.

If my father would only hire somebody competent and reliable to go shopping with him for a week's worth of Good Food groceries, I wouldn't have to spend my Saturday mornings and afternoons in this side of D.C. shopping for collard greens, cans of mackerel, blocks of lard, and frozen pigs' feet, ankles, intestines, and ears. I wouldn't have to listen to those men standing around in their suspicious circle in front of Sol Sanders & Sons getting hungry cannibal looks in their eyes, damning every time a woman walked by. Talking "hey man gotta get 'tween those legs, move on in smooth and slow," and giving their crotches a congratulatory tug or two. Two of them had leaned against my father's truck, looked inside, and asked me if I got the time. Why you giving me that Chinese look like you can't speak no English? You Chinese? No, I am not Chinese, nor am I Japanese, Taiwanese, Vietnamese, dirty knees or look at these. I am a Korean-American. They sneered at me with their what-the-difference look. The difference is as apparent as night and day, rich and poor, salvation and damnation, heaven and hell, awareness and ignorance, literate and illiterate, you and me.

Instead, in a feeble voice I mumbled it was almost one o'clock. One of them told me to speak up 'cause he couldn't hear me, so I held up my index finger and pointed to the sky.

If only my father would hire good help.

But when he did hire someone, he hired the wrong

kind of help. Remember Donna? Donna May Johnson was not the type of person one would take into employment. Father said she was a strong girl and could lift two boxes of sodas and a slab of bacon at the same time. But she was a thief and a liar. She hid packs of Camels in her waistband underneath her apron. She had wads and wads of our napkins stuffed in her purse. She drank as many sodas as her strong arms could carry. And guess in whose kitchen our coffeemaker perks coffee? Still he would not fire her.

Because of her, *I* had to boil pig ankle, pig feet, pig neck, pig ear, pig skin all last summer because his hired help with the strong biceps and deltoids wanted to take a week off to take her two sons to Disneyland. Didn't my father know her boyfriend had moved to Florida four days before that? When Donna never showed up that Monday, he called home from the store telling me to get up, get ready because he was coming to get me. Did he not know I had books to read, thoughts to jot down, my moral view of the universe to form, the truth of the human condition to contemplate, a creative fire to fan, art to serve . . . ? He came, got me, and all last summer I learned lima beans taste good with two chunks of lard in the soup, Grand Northern beans taste good with pieces of fatback floating in the juices, pinto beans taste good plain, and everything tastes good with hot sauce.

I learned to scramble Davey's eggs while spreading grape jelly and melted butter on Hugo's biscuit. I knew everyone took ketchup and hot sauce on their home fries except Mr. Selby and Joe from Joe's Body Shop next door. Mr. Selby took honey in his morning coffee because sugar made his hands shake, and honey, you can't have shaking hands if you're going to drive a limo all day, you know what I mean? And Jamie came in at 2:12 for a medium-sized Styrofoam bowl of spaghetti, ate it at the table, and lingered around thinking I'd give him more if he eyed the steam table long enough. "Hey, Mr. Cho, this here your son?" He looked down at my chest and could see that through my thin white T-shirt, I happened to be wearing a bra. "Damn, I thought you were—excuse me." And his girlfriend gave a huh-huh of a laugh.

I went to the back room where the sodas were stored, stood on top of the boxes, cursed Donna May, her boyfriend, her two sons, and the entire state of Florida, prayed for a miraculous enlightenment that would convince Father to terminate her employment, pointed two forefingers at my temples and commanded my hair to grow, grow, grow because not only was I a Korean-American, I was a Korean-American woman.

Donna May called the following Friday and told my father to send her check to her new Florida address. She also said that she would appreciate it if he could write a nice reference letter about how she was a dependable employee because she was applying for a position as cook at an all-you-can-eat restaurant underneath the Sandy Shore Hotel. Why didn't he write them the truth? Why did he tell them she was good help, good cook, good girl, while complaining to me how she always cook biscuit too long black bottom crazy girl and never call never call when she going to be late and she alway late, one day her boy got a flu, other day her other boy got a stomachache, and other day she catch her boy flu, and she sick. She never cook fatback right. Boil hog maw too little time. Customers all the time complaining hog maw too tough, hog maw too tough. Just like the rubber band.

I had to stay the rest of the summer until Connie got hired and trained.

Father turned to me and insisted, "Angela mom store not here."

"What are you talking about? Thirteen more minutes down this street and Sunny Grocery stands on your right."

"Her store in northeast."

"Northeast, southwest, northwest, who cares?"

"Her store in northeast."

"All right. All right. Her store's in northeast."

"This is southeast," he said.

"Whatever," I said, and scratched off a patch of dried grease on the dashboard. "Abba, don't forget to buy a box of King Edward cigars."

During that summer, Mr. Stuart came in for cigars and a turkey salad on wheat toast, hold the onions please. He asked me how old I was, what grade I was in, and what I wanted to be when I got older. He told me I was a bright young lady and he would talk to my boss about giving me the rest of the summer off. I told him my father was in the process of hiring new help, that he was presently undergoing a vigorous search for a competent and reliable employee. Mr. Stuart always walked out of the store with sandwich and cigar in hand looking back at me like I was wasting my life in front of a grill. I thought Connie would take over the grill, but she only brought bad luck.

On her first day, when I was showing her how to scramble eggs, spread butter and jelly on a biscuit, and take the next order at the same time, she was pouring coffee into her Styrofoam cup. She didn't stop pouring until the hot black liquid spilled over onto her hand. She dropped the cup. She dropped the coffeepot. I slipped on the puddle and glass trying to reach the rags next to the sink. My forearms landed on the grill. The two men waiting to give their orders laughed. The rest of the day Connie had to figure her own way around the steam table, while I soaked my arms in a bucket of cold water. I was grilled for life.

The next day my father came home from Good Food with thick gauze wrapped around the middle finger of his right hand. Connie couldn't pick up the box of plastic wrap to place on top of the shelf next to the stack of eggs. He told me she had said, "Mr. Cho, Mr. Cho, you got to help me." He picked it up, but the box was covered with grease from Connie's bacon-slicing hands, so it slipped down. The serrated edge slipped down and cut right through the flesh of his middle finger. I told him to get rid of Connie.

"Dad, Angela's mother isn't even in the store on Saturdays," I said now.

"Oh yeah, she open on Saturday," he said.

"I know, but she doesn't come in on Saturdays. She has people taking care of the store on Saturdays."

"Her store busy on Saturday."

"I know her store's busy, but she's not there."

"Most customers come in Saturdays."

"You're absolutely right about that. Her store is busy on Saturdays," I agreed.

My father handed me a torn piece of paper with our grocery list written on it.

Steak was spelled "stek"; Coke was spelled "cok"; collard greens was "collar greens"; cabbage was missing a b; and rice was spelled with an l. My father was spelling all his words incorrectly. When would he learn that steak had a long "a" sound with a silent e? He had to understand that collars were flaps around the necks of shirts, blouses, jackets, and coats. Collars weren't greens. And our customers would die if we steamed and served lice. They would just die. And it wasn't, What it is. It was, What is it. What is it? What is it?

My father had to learn. He had to learn that he just could not trust any man who walked into the carry-out bearing what looked like boxes of brand-new Sony videocassette recorders. Even though they were only $100 each and he bargained the price down to $75, he should not have trusted them. I knew he was thinking, One for Ahn Joo's room, one for his room when he bought two for $150 and thought it a steal. But couldn't he tell immediately that those pictures pasted on the boxes were magazine cutouts?

He didn't even shut his car door that day because he was too excited about showing me his steal. He called from the garage, "Joo-yah, Joo-yah!" and when I didn't answer, he came into my room with the two unopened boxes and placed them in the middle of my floor. I handed him a pair of scissors and he began to cut through the masking tape. Didn't he know that brand-new Sony VCRs were not packaged with masking tape? He opened it, and we found a plastic bag full of dirt, pieces of glass, jagged rocks, bottlecaps, and cigarette butts. And he actually had the heart to open the second box hoping that that one was for real. . . .

After reading the shopping list, I said, "I thought you were going to get all the sodas delivered?"

"We buy RC," he said.

"Those bottles are too heavy for you to carry. You're going to break your back."

"I can carry."

"It's because of the delivery man, isn't it? You didn't like him and you couldn't call them to ask for another delivery person. Is that it?" I asked.

"It's not heavy."

"Dad, you're their customer. You know you can complain and request a different delivery person," I said.

"It's all right. I can take care of it. I can take care," he sang, and turned right driving through an open fence holding the "WELCOME TO FLORIDA MARKET—WASHINGTON—CASH-&-CARRY" sign. Behind the fence were rows of wholesale warehouses: Sol Sanders & Sons, Meat Wholesale, Bretcher's Beef, Nello's Candies & Notions, and all the other stores we needed to go to. Load and unload. Load and unload, that was what he needed me for.

He drove between the parked vans and trucks and stopped in front of Sol Sanders & Sons. He turned off the ignition, pulled the parking brake, tossed his sunglasses on the dashboard, opened his door, spat out some phlegm, said, "Stay here," and shut the door. I watched his short figure walk toward the heavy plastic strips that hung as drapes at the entrance of the store. He flung them back. He faded in with the voices of Mr. Sanders and his sons.

I leaned my back against the door, straightened out my legs onto the driver's seat, and hung my head outside. I told him to check all the potatoes for eyes before he buys the entire bag. Eyes made the potato a pain to peel.

The sun felt hot on my forehead and nose. One of the four men near the door was finishing a bag of potato chips. He shook the remains into his opened mouth and crumpled up the bag. I tasted the salt in my own mouth and felt thirsty for the man.

A heavy African woman wearing a bright yellow and brown dress with an African print stood behind a table of stacked tapes between two huge, silent speakers. She shaded her eyes from the sun, looked my way, and waved her hand for me to come and buy her tapes. But I closed my eyes. Her figure was dancing to African voodoo music in my mind. As the oppressive drumbeats quickened, she pranced around a fire that gradually died down. And as the fire gradually died down, her dress transformed into a red and green *hanbok,* her head now covered in white cloth, and with her long white sleeves she spun fluttering rings. The deep drumbeats changed into the sound of clanging cymbals, and the woman swayed in the center of the busy marketplace in the village of the One Hundred-Year-Old Mountain, where a fishmonger, basket weaver, and kelp seller's loud bargaining with customers competed with the shaman's chanting.

From the back of the truck, my father called, "Joo-yah!" I saw him signal with his right hand for me to come around, unload the cart, and help him load the bed of his truck.

A crate of Twin Shields collard greens, a sack of Kings potatoes, and a sack of Sylvany Spanish onions.

"Did you check to see if the potatoes had eyes?" I asked.

"They got no eyes," he said.

"Did you check to see if they were rotten? Remember the last time? Some of them were purple, bruised up."

"Guh reh. Guh reh."

"Did you get the biggest onions? You know how hard they are to slice if they're the size of golf balls. They don't even stay on the slicing machine."

"Guh reh."

"Dad, this isn't a smart idea at all. We should have gotten the vegetables last. They're probably going to wilt in this weather."

"Go inside. Too many words today. You got too many words."

I had too many words? He was the one with too many words. And they were all inappropriate ones. I told him not to talk like his customers, damning and hey manning and what you doing with my eggs, little miss, and if you ever thinking about getting married mmm mmm mmm. I told him to refuse the girlie magazines, postcards, and calendars the mechanic next door gave him. Didn't he remember what they did to

Mother? He didn't have to take them. He could simply say, no thank you, instead of stashing them underneath the cash register and taking a peek at them when the lunch crowd died down. Or stashing the cutouts in the Yellow Pages or the Korean phone directory or between the pages of *Yes, You Too Can Speak English, Too.*

Only three words. No—thank—you. No thank you. He had no trouble saying them when I cooked him brown rice with beans instead of the white rice because brown rice was better for one's digestion and had more nutrients, or when I served him pasta shells with marinara instead of *gook soo,* lettuce with vinegar and oil instead of *kimchi.* He wanted red meat so I cooked steak, but he wanted *kal bi.* No thank you; he said it to me easily.

My father parked in front of Deck-Bone Cash & Carry, and I said, "Dad, don't go to Deck-Bone Cash & Carry."

"Deck-Bone is cheap," he said.

"I know, but they don't carry everything, which means we'll have to go to two meat stores today."

"Shut up. We go to three today," he said.

He should have gone to Meat Time Eat Time instead of Deck-Bone Cash & Carry because Deck-Bone didn't carry chicken gizzards. Chicken gizzards with gravy over rice, although a little expensive, went over especially well on Thursdays because Thursday was payday for the Navy Yard workers. But my father never listened to me.

He went ahead, got out of the car, shut the door, put the shopping list in his back pocket, pulled his socks up, walked into Deck-Bone, and looked for his frozen turkey wings, ham hock, and slab of bacon. He was not going to find any chicken gizzards in there.

Minutes later, my father tapped my window with his knuckles and said, "Come on." I followed him to the back where a cartload of everything they like to eat was waiting for me to unload. The customers loved Juicy Fruit chewing gum. They loved orange-flavored Nehi and grape-flavored Rock Creek. Salmon cake made of canned mackerel and breadcrumbs. Salt and vinegar and barbeque on everything. Deep-fried pig skin chips and hot potato sticks.

We finally arrived back at the store, and Father backed the truck to Good Food's front door. He opened the bars, unbolted the top, middle, and two bottom locks, pulled open the door, and pushed the screen back, hooking the handle on a rusty bent nail. I crawled into the bed of the truck and waited for him to bring the cart so I could load and he could roll the boxes and sacks to the back. But he didn't come out like he usually did with a smile or a burp or a scratch. He didn't come out. So I called him three times. When he didn't answer, I worried, remembering how Angela's father got stabbed. I climbed out of the truck and looked inside.

My father was on his hands and knees picking up the quarters, dimes, nickels, and pennies that had spilled out of the cash register when the burglars cracked open the drawer. He collected the coins into the King Edward cigar box. The chairs were knocked over onto the middle of the floor. Tables turned.

Greasy posters of cheeseburgers and french fries hanging by one corner. Cigarette cartons torn and stepped on. Clean napkins scattered on the floor, like they had been thrown up in the air by gloved hands. I could see them having a party in here. One with chunks of ham and roast beef, one with a carton of beer, one with the slicing machine coming in and going out of the hole they had drilled in the middle of our wall underneath our sink next to our steam table in front of the grill. The only things left in the back were opened sacks of cornmeal, mousetraps, and the stink of horse manure from Mr. Selby's limo service. They were renting out horse, carriage, and rider by the hour because the weather was so pleasant nowadays.

When a path was finally cleared, I wheeled the cart around from the storage room to the back of the truck. My father was mopping up the eggshells. I loaded the cart with stacked boxes of bottled orange and grape-flavored RC. I rolled the cart to the back. He was still mopping up the eggshells. I unloaded the cart and rolled it back to the truck. Sylvany Spanish onions wheeled to the cooking room; Kings potatoes leaned against the onions; the crate of collard greens in the refrigerator. He picked up the napkins, dusted them on his thigh, and collected them in a pile. I loaded the cart with turkey wings, ham hock, and the slab of bacon. I rolled the cart to the freezer and unloaded. He was taping the greasy posters back up on the wall. I rolled the cart back to the truck, unloaded the boxes of Snickers, Milky Ways, Three Musketeers, M&Ms, and five boxes of Juicy Fruit, the gum they love to chew, and wheeled them to the counter. He was looking into the hole, shaking his balding head, and touching the edges of the circle they made. I wheeled the empty cart to the back storage room and leaned it against the wall underneath the light switch.

I swept the floors, while he tried to cover up the hole by nailing a piece of plywood over it. I swept the corners, underneath the tables and counters, and around his stooped body. We wouldn't be able to total up the week's worth of sales on the cash register. I mopped. I poured Clorox and Ajax into the bucket of hot water, dunked the mop in, and without wringing it, dripped the water onto the floor. I scrubbed the corners, underneath the tables and counters, and around his stooped body. I wrung the mop and soaked up the soapy water from the wet floor. The mop slapped.

I washed and rinsed the four coffeepots, using rags rubber-banded around the tip of a tong. He was still nailing the piece of plywood over the hole. I dried the coffeepots and returned them to the coffeemaker.

I scraped the week's worth of grease into the large can that held a month's worth of grease. I shut it and wobbled out to the alley with it. When I returned, he had finished nailing the piece of plywood over the hole. I rinsed out the toilet bowl. I emptied out the trash. I beat the dust out of the welcome mat.

My father spoke in Korean. *"Ahn Joo-yah, let's go home."*

He locked the four bolts and let the door of bars clank shut. It shut, and we heard liquid quickly streaming. When we looked into the alley, there was an old black man peeing next to our can of a month's worth of grease. When my father quickly turned me around and pushed me toward the truck, I heard the man say he was sorry, but he couldn't help it, you know how it is. My father said he was sorry and hey man you can finish, take your time. The man zipped up and walked to the end of the alley.

My father sat on the driver's seat and fiddled with the gear before starting the ignition. I looked at him and said, "What the hell is his problem? Can't he find another hole to land his pee?"

He didn't answer. He drove over a curb, barely missing the NO PARKING sign that was bent in a forty-five-degree angle.

"Dad, who does he think he is?" I screamed.

My father told me to quiet down.

"It's bad enough Mr. Selby's horses shit there, why does he have hang his dick and piss in our alley? I can't stand this. I can't stand it. It's making me sick. It's bad enough we get robbed, why does he have to add on to our misery and leave his urine in our alley? That's illegal, do you know that?"

He opened the glove compartment and took out a napkin to wipe off the sweat beading on his head.

In Korean he said, *"Ahn Joo-yah, please let's drive home quietly."*

I wanted to tell him the robbery and the urine were absolute injustices, we were wronged, and the guilty would eventually have to pay their karma debt. All of them. For stabbing Angela's father, for holding Yoo Jin's mother at gunpoint underneath the toilet, for shooting off Mr. Hong's ear for a couple of hundred dollars and a bag of chips, for calling Mrs. Kim a stingy money-hungry chink because she refused to give her customers cleaning for free or because she charged extra for boxed shirts, for making me write badly to save myself from being accused of copying out of a book, for telling me to go back to where I came from (how can I return to my mother's womb?), for stretching their large, long, curly-lashed eyes at me while singing about my being Chinese and Japanese, for making me want to look, walk, eat, sleep, talk like them, for expecting me to sit quietly in the back of the classroom, for making me repeat my question two or three times because no one could hear my voice squeezed out of a throat that always had clay caught in the center except when it was speaking to Father. When I spoke at Father, my throat opened up and clever words, sentences, paragraphs came to me. It was because I believed I knew better than he.

He had pushed his socks down to his ankles because the weather was warm, and the vent above the pedals blew air. The vinyl seats were sticking to my thighs. The sun reflected off the side of a high rise made of mirrors that twinkled, blinked, and winked at me as if trying to dazzle me to keep its secrets. We were driving across a bridge over a river. The wind beat in and made noise. But it didn't keep me from hearing my father's breathing, which was his pathetic plea: *Ahn Joo-yah, Ahn Joo-yah, you have to save your poor father. You are the reason I do this. I cannot do this for long. Study hard, place first in your class, become a doctor or lawyer, take care of me, make money, make my suffering pay off, make my sacrifice worthwhile . . .*

A man on a ten-speed carrying a blue knapsack on his back pedaled past us as my father slowed down to exit the bridge. As he switched gears, I saw my hand zigzag and tremble next to his, bound at the wrist by steel rings.

Duty caught me by the throat, keeping me from beating my forehead against the bathroom floor as my mother used to do while she chanted and wailed: *Why did you bring me to this awful, awful country?*

13

It was almost three in the morning, and I was reading about metal knees, plastic hearts, motorized elbows, and electronic ears replacing damaged or missing pieces of the human body, remembering Boris, and thinking of turning the radio on low and slow-dancing with my pillow, when the telephone rang. My father's oldest brother from Pusan, who had never contacted us since our family immigrated to America, was calling to inform him that their father had passed away from a long-term illness. Something had been terminally wrong with his male organ for years now. To them, the death did not come as a surprise. He lived some years more than they had expected. Everyone here is fine. Are you fine? I'm fine. We're fine. And my father threw the phone on the floor, returned to his pillow, mumbled something about how unlucky it was to get calls in the middle of the night, and in a matter of seconds, he was snoring again.

"Daddy, are you all right?" I asked. "Do you want me to get you anything? Anything at all?" My father told me to be quiet and go back to sleep.

I returned to my room, thinking that my grandfather's death was a relief for the both of us. He had done enough damage in his lifetime, beating the sanity out of his own daughter, beating and driving my father out of his own country, and stashing his first wife away in some remote village. Who knows how he got rid of his second wife? My father told me that when he visited his mother before leaving for America, she had given him one dried red pepper as a farewell gift, shown him off to the other villagers as her son the doctor in the city, having confused him with her other sons, and offered him dinner while smearing her own feces on walls. My grandfather's judgment day was long overdue, I told myself as I turned on the radio, took a gentle hold of my pillow, and slow-danced with Ian Krauss, my lab science partner and make-believe boyfriend.

For Sunday breakfast, I made my father soybean soup with tofu cubes, squash, and mushrooms, and laid a fried egg on top of his rice. Our retired neighbor, Mr. Smith, was mowing his lawn again, the second time this week, and the our-three-sons neighbor had the sprinkler going over their garden with its tomatoes, cucumbers, and daffodils. While waiting for my father to come downstairs for his meal, I looked out of our kitchen window and watched the Korean grandmother hang long strips of nylon gauze to dry on her clothesline.

Their deck was twice the size of ours. They had a gas grill on which the grandmother cooked croakers and barbecued marinated beef for her daughter-in-law, who was pregnant with her oldest son's first child. Once, I tried to greet the grandmother, and she asked me in Korean if I was Chinese.

"I was born in Pusan," I assured her.

"Your father's Chinese, isn't he? No? Then, your mother, she's got to be Chinese. One of them has to be Chinese because those eyes, those eyes aren't Korean eyes. The shape of your face, your hair, even the way you blink. It's not Korean. Let me ask you something," she said, squinting her eyes at me. And when she asked me if American girls menstruated, I firmly told her that menstruation was not a matter of race or culture, and ran back home before she could ask me if I had started mine.

Standing at the bottom of the stairs, I yelled up that the soup was getting cold and the egg on the rice was beginning to freeze. "Hurry up and come down. At this rate, I'll be making lunch in another hour."

I heard the garage door open, followed by the sound of the sliding door of my father's van. He had woken up early, driven to Good Food for his electric drill, saw, and favorite hammer, and stopped off at a hardware store for two-by-fours, screws, nails, and a twenty-five-foot chain to build a swing set for two in our backyard.

"There's no room for this," I said.

"Oh sure. Plenty of room," he said, carrying his toolbox to the back.

"Where? Where're you going to put it?"

"I'm going to hang on cherry tree."

"Yeah, and break your neck," I said. "Dad, that's my favorite tree. Don't kill it."

"Don't worry. I'm not going to kill, silly girl," he said, and went back to the van for his two-by-fours.

"There's soup on the table."

"I eat already," he said.

Sound was coming from every part of our street. If not my father's drilling, hammering, and sawing, then it was the honking cars lined up bumper to bumper on Morning Glory Way trying to find parking for the softball tournaments held at Weston, and the children whose laughter and whining seemed to resonate underneath the heat of the sun, and the lawn mowers that seemed to turn on and off in swift succession. Feeling a little left out, I decided to contribute to the neighborhood noise by vacuuming, running the washer, dryer, and dishwasher, reciting the definition of ten more SAT words, and playing a tune or two on the piano during commercial breaks before running my Sunday evening bath.

I was trying to curl my hair with a hot iron when my father called me from outside to take a look, to take a ride.

"Dad, it doesn't look very stable," I said, brushing my damp hair behind the kitchen screen door.

"Oh sure, it's stable. It's strong," he said, as he sat down and swung back and forth. Gripping the chain, he pushed his feet against the grass, and the swing swung higher. "You can try," he said, waving his free hand and patting the wooden seat where I was to sit next to him.

I told him it would never hold two people, my hair was still wet, the hot iron was on, and I had to warm up the leftover soup for dinner. As I left him on his swing and returned upstairs, I started to feel the way I had some months ago after freeing the brown rabbit my father had trapped and caged in our backyard. I had found my father in his room with his head down on his desk, listening to an opera, and tried to explain in my best Korean that the poor rabbit was better off free, on its own, with its family, with other rabbits. I asked him how he could possibly watch the poor thing mutilate its own face trying to escape through the bars and wires his hands had built. He told me it wasn't my rabbit to free. I hadn't trapped it. I hadn't fed it carrots and lettuce leaves every morning. I hadn't cleaned its cage. I hadn't rubbed ointment on its wounds. He said that when he was a boy, he had taken care of plenty of rabbits in Korea, and he was planning on letting it go once its wounds healed. He said a rabbit in that condition would surely die by the end of the day. He told me to go outside and clean up its mess.

That evening, I had taken apart my father's handiwork. It was a beautiful cage with a wooden frame, sanded corners, a door with hinges, a bed of spinach, lettuce, and dandelion leaves, and a shingled roof to shield the rabbit from the sun and rain.

Finally, our street was quiet, and I could hear Mr. Smith's telephone ringing. After heating the soup, I went outside to the swing set, where my father was oiling the metal rings from which the chains hung. He said it was squeaking a bit. There were white *salonpas* patches on the back of his neck, behind his left ear, and on his right elbow. When he wore one on the back of his neck, it meant his head was aching.

Sitting in the middle of the swing seat, I said, "Dinner's ready."

My father put down the oilcan and pushed me from behind. "I'll push it higher," he said.

"Stop, I'm going to throw up," I said and hopped off.

Stopping the swing, he got on himself, and told me to sit by him. I could smell the menthol of the *salonpas* patches and noticed that my father was beginning to bald. Crickets were singing to each other. Traces of conversation came from another backyard, and someone was having a barbecue. The swing set faced my father's garden, and I stared at the patch of perilla leaves, squash, tomatoes, and the single eggplant that looked like a big fat purple teardrop. When he pushed his feet against the grass to swing a little higher, I told him the tree would come crashing down on us, roots and all. As he yawned and rubbed his left eye with his thumb, he told me that when he was a boy in Korea, he had built a swing out of nothing but a piece of rope and some branches. He had built it on the cypress tree next to the village well.

There were many stories about the village well: drownings of newborns, drownings of virgins, spirits that rose from its water, faces that appeared on its surface. My father could have built his swing on the apple tree that grew on his family's farm, but his stepmother wouldn't let him. She was afraid he would snatch an apple and have one less to sell at the market. The apples grew as large as a man's fists, and they tasted sweet. My father had stolen one the night a fire broke out in another villager's outhouse. He had dug a hole in the ground, lined it with flat rocks, and hid the apple that needed a day to ripen. When he returned to the hole, a juicy red apple awaited him. It was the only time he had eaten from his family's apple tree.

"My oldest brother, the one who called, he tried to eat from that tree, but our stepmother caught him and he was beaten badly. He simply stood there, not saying a word, taking the beating. He never fought back.

He couldn't even walk straight for a week. I think that's how he got his stutter."

My father held onto to the chain and stared down into his garden. It was getting dark, and I could see the calendar hanging on our refrigerator door in the lighted kitchen. Hearing the sound of an airplane flying over us, my father said that it always excited him to hear an airplane passing by. When he was a boy and war planes flew over his village, he would point to the sky and scream out, "It's the nose people, it's the nose people!" because Americans had such tall and pointy noses. When my father was sixteen years old, he had an American pen pal, Naomi Jordan of Oklahoma City, Oklahoma. On her birthday, he had sent her a compact and lipstick. He had kept her letters. Her handwriting was beautiful. Before my father could turn to me and beg me to track her down for him, I got off the swing and said that dinner was getting cold, and the soup was no good if more than a day old.

Catching me by the wrist, my father asked me if I had written anything. I told him I was working on my longest story and had written more than half of it already.

"Go get it. Let me hear it," he said.

"I can't read it out here. It's too dark."

"Then you turn the light on when you come back."

"Dad, it's not finished yet. It's not that good."

"Let me hear it," he said, and smiled at me.

When I returned to the swing with my pages of writing, my father was holding the eggplant in his hand. He said that if it grew too large, the skin would toughen and its insides would go bitter, that we had to eat it while it was tender and sweet. As I held my pages underneath our deck light and shooed off mosquitos and gnats, I told my father the story wasn't finished yet, and if anything sounded confusing, to stop me.

"Just read," he said.

"All right," I said. I cleared my throat to read aloud to my father what I had written so far: "A village schoolteacher calling roll in front of his class of children whose parents were rice, barley, potato, or rabbit farmers threw his chalk at the boy in the back, who never washed, never wore shoes, and had already fallen asleep next to his puddle of drool."

"Where's school?" my father interrupted.

"In Korea. You've got to hear the rest of it, though. Just wait. It comes up in the next sentence," I said, and continued. "The chalk hit the shoulder of the sleeping boy's desk partner whose older brother had run away to Seoul to make a life for himself in the city because the filthy country was only full of dirt-work, pulling and planting and eating weeds that grew out of cow dung, and he wanted to work in a government office. Many of the young men and women villagers wanted to work in a government office, especially the women who had finished high school, but could not go on to college. They wanted to be typists or copiers and maybe meet a higher-ranking office worker who was still a bachelor. They could marry, live in one of the new high-rise apartments in Seoul, and have a child or two. What an impossible dream! Either that or meet an American man while working as a typist in an army office, the way one young woman did, except she married a black man, and her mother and father would not let her enter the village or enter the house, not even for a visit, because marrying an American was one thing—but a black man? She was locked out. So the black man took his new wife to America, where they lived in a high-rise apartment with a balcony overlooking streets, cars, people, a purple mountain and a raging sea. There were many women who married American men."

"Do you want to marry American man?" my father interrupted.

"Dad, that's what you told me. It's not about me. Do you want me to read or not?" I asked.

He nodded for me to continue. "There were many women who married American men. And if they had younger sisters, the girls tried on their lace underwear and slips and smeared Pond's Cold Cream on their faces, necks, arms, and legs, thinking it was lotion, and besides, anything made in America was good for you. Even the peasants with squash-shaped heads knew that. American chewing gum, American cola, American cigarettes were worth a month's worth of wages. If the teacher were to ask his students what they wanted to do when they were older, they would answer, either work as a clerk for the government or become a nurse, doctor, or teacher or live in America. Nobody wanted to be a farmer, potter, sea diver, fishmonger, or popcorn, fruit, rubber shoe seller like their mothers and fathers, who began work before the sun rose and came home to a bowl of barley, a basket of lettuce, bean paste sauce, and a pot of lukewarm cabbage soup after the sun set. In the winter, they ate inside on the heated floor. In spring, summer, and fall, they ate outside on the veranda, while watching uncle climb a crooked ladder to patch a hole in the thatched roof, little brother chase a rat, and mother with food in her mouth yell at them to come and eat the meal she had cooked. The uncle wasn't hungry. . . ."

I stopped, noticing my father was yawning. I told him the soup was surely cold by now and my throat was dry from the reading. "Let's go inside. I'll finish it later," I said.

"If it's cold, then it's cold. Just finish it right now," he said. "Just finish it."

I skipped a page and read about a young woman. "The young woman was a bit uncertain and hesitant, but she did not show it because she loved the young man, who was so eager to please her. Caressing her cheek, he said he would take care of her, take her away from her father and four brothers, who only made her work. He kissed her coarse hands, telling her she was made for more than farm and housework. Farm and housework was not the reason one mother was packing her bags to leave her husband and two daughters. While her daughters were at school and her husband at work in the rice mill, she stayed home and drank bowls of expensive coffee until a well-dressed man in eyeglasses, a silk tie, and polished shoes knocked at her gate to use her telephone. He told her she was beautiful and asked if he could join her for a cup of coffee. She was restless and lonely and tired of being teased by her friends because her husband worked in a rice mill. She wanted to live a bigger life. So she let the man return to the house two, three, four times, and when he told her he had to go tend to his orchard of orange trees on Cheju Island, she said she would follow him. She would follow him anywhere. 'Please let me go with you,' she begged him in a low whisper, which he could hardly hear because the old woman next door was wailing about her oldest son, who had died of a heart attack a week ago. The mother wailed, while a boy three houses away yelled from outside his gate, 'I am a thief. I am a thief. I am a thief,' as a punishment from his father for having stolen his stepmother's gold ring. He wanted to trade it for comic books, chewing gum, Popsicles, and a kite that would surely fly higher than any of the other boys' in the village.

"Fly high, high, high, swooping over the peak of the One-Hundred-Year-Old Mountain, where a temple was carved on its sloping side. A Buddha with smooth stone joints sat erect, looking down on the three piles of carefully stacked pebbles beside its left knee. On the second step of the tile-roofed temple housing the monks lay a row of white rubber shoes. The servant, who was a seventeen-year-old girl, swept those steps of the leaves that fell in autumn, snow in winter, and rain in spring. She walked with a limp and suffered pain when she had to straighten her back to light the candles on the high shelves. She was told suffering would purify her soul. So, when she waited for the large pot of rice to finish steaming to feed the monks with and remembered her poor mother, she sighed and tried to hold back her tears for the sake of her soul. Her poor mother. She remembered how her father had pulled her mother by the hair, dragging her body toward the door because she had sneaked out of the house in the afternoon to meet her friends, who laughed, sang, imitated their husbands, and told stories. She had worn her colorful clothes beneath the gray full-length skirt and heavy sweater, pretending to go to market, but turned the corner into her friend's house, where the music came from.

"When the servant girl saw her mother last, she was counting and recounting the five dried red peppers laid out on her skirt, dividing them among her invisible friends and telling stories about her son, who was a famous doctor in the city. She said he was coming to visit her, and when he came, she would take him around the village from door to door to show him off because he was a handsome man. She had no sons. Like the mother of four daughters, who rubbed her hands under the moon praying the fifth child would be a boy or else her mother-in-law would demand her husband take another woman, who was able to bear him a son. The oldest daughter cut her and her sisters' hair to boys' length and told them to deepen their voices because it was their faults their mother threw up all her food.

"The mother finally had her son, but soon after the birth, she left her five children and husband to live on Cheju Island as a sea diver for oysters, clams, sea cucumbers, and worms. She was losing her hearing. The silence at the bottom of the sea met her on land, and she could not hear the prices her customers called out. She read their lips. In a loud voice, she called out a more reasonable price. Her children were forgotten in the sea. 'From sea to shining sea' were the words to an

American song one woman had learned while living with an American man in the basement of a house owned by an elderly couple, who lived upstairs and constantly told her how beautiful her hair was. But mice lived in the basement as well, and they reminded her of the huge rats at the orphanage that bit her in her sleep. Whenever she heard scratching or squeaking, she jumped on the bed, slapping her face as if fighting off crawling insects and screaming for her mother in Korean.

"At first, the American man was understanding. He gently held and rocked her to sleep, calling her his baby, sweet little baby, there, there, you're safe in my arms. But after a few months, he grew tired of her broken English, her broken ways, and got into the habit of striking her whenever she jumped on the bed. When that didn't stop her outbursts, he held a mouse by its tail over her head, threatening to drop it on her beautiful hair if she didn't shut the hell up because she was giving him a fucking headache. During those nights, she tried to remember the face of her elder sister, who she dreamed was eating delicious foods and wearing pretty dresses, living in a house of her own. And she hoped to see her again someday, which was unlikely because her sister had returned to Korea to a remote village in a country and worked in a winehouse, entertaining men with her piano playing, singing, and if they were willing to pay, a private room for the night. It rarely happened that a winehouse girl met a man who would marry her, but she did because she happened to know the music and words to his favorite song: 'I'm just a lonely boy, lonely and blue, I'm all alone with nothing to do. . . . All I want is someone to love, someone to kiss, someone to hold, somebody, somebody, somebody, please. . . .' "

My father's eyes were closed, and the night wind was gently swinging us. I tapped him on the shoulder. When he opened his eyes, I told him that was all I had written so far, that I tried to get everything he had told me down, that my throat was hurting, and I was hungry. He nodded in agreement, and we walked into our kitchen.

The next morning, my father did not go into the store and I did not go to school because on his chest, right over his heart, and all across his left side, ending at the center of his spine, were red, inflamed lesions. The pain would not let my father move. He told me to boil dandelion leaves, take him to his acupuncturist, and hang a crucifix on the center of his headboard.

I drove him from doctor to doctor. Those Korean doctors could not tell us what the hell was wrong with him; they said he had liver problems, indigestion, maybe preliminary signs of heart disease, allergies, a pulled muscle from his daily sit-ups, too much stress from work. At the end of the day, I drove him to the emergency room at the hospital, and as we waited, I told my father that this was all because of Grandfather. "He's haunting you," I said. "You've got to get him out. You've got to talk him out. He's an asshole. Talk about it." He answered me with a one-syllable grunt, in agreement or disagreement or simply to shut me up.

A bearded doctor examined my father and diagnosed him with shingles. Shingles! What a lovely simple sound. It rhymed with jingles, tingles, mingles. Shingles was not a terminal or dangerous disease. It was caused by stress or fatigue, a reawakening of a chicken pox virus living in the bloodstream infecting the nervous system. It was a simple and common virus, the nurse explained. The lesions and the pain would vanish in two weeks.

My father, lying on the tissue-covered bed with his hand over his heart, helplessly repeated to the nurse, "I'm so scared for tonight. It's so painful, so very painful. How can I sleep?"

I listened carefully to my father as I sat on the plastic chair next to the stainless-steel sink underneath a box of rubber gloves that hung from the wall. Under my breath, I was urging him in Korean to tell the nurse about his father's death. Tell her everything. Tell her what an asshole he was. The shingles was caused by the news of his father's death. Instead, my father was asking the nurse if he could be operated on to get rid of the awful pain. She said an operation was unnecessary, and he would be given a prescription for painkillers.

I wanted to hear him say, "It is so painful, so very painful. I am scared for tonight. I cannot sleep. You see, my father has died, and I cannot get myself to do the right thing, which is to go to Korea, which is to go to his funeral. My father has died. All day long, I have been hearing his voice in my ears. His voice rings in my ears. My father's last words to me were spoken on the telephone. He told me to have a good life. The way you Americans say it to people you don't ever want to see for the rest of your life. He told me to have a good life. I will not go to his funeral. I have no excuse. The only thing that keeps me here in America like a coward is hatred. You see, I hate my father because when I was a boy, he sent me into the fields to work while my brothers were sent to school. They all live well in Korea. He beat me. He would not buy me shoes. He would not let me eat eggs, which he said were too good for me. It was because of him that my sister is living in a Buddhist temple, a little crazy in the head, that my blood mother is living alone in a village, very much crazy in the head. On my wedding day, he struck me across my ear so hard that when I was walking down the aisle to meet my bride, my ears were ringing. I could not hear the music. I could not hear her vows. She is no longer with us. She took my son and returned to Korea. I ran away to America because of my father. He was so bad to me. I do not know why. I do not understand. And now, now, now, my father is dead. It is so painful. I am scared of tonight because the pain will be most agonizing in the night on my bed when my clock blinks two fifty-five."

I imagined hearing my father saying these words in perfect English or broken, I did not care, in tears or with a smile, I did not care. He was saying them to the bearded doctor and the nurse who spoke slowly and clearly when she explained that shingles was not dangerous. In my perfect world, they would have listened and been moved by my father's story. I imagined they were moved to tears. But the visit ended with a morphine shot, and I led my dizzy and babbling father out of the hospital.

At home, when I put him to bed, my father cried and mumbled that he loved all his brothers, would lay his life down for them, would send them all the money that they wanted in the world, and as he started to mumble something about Min Joo and my mother, I walked toward the door. He called out, "Joo-yah."

"Dad, what can I get you?"

"Joo-yah," he cried.

"Dad, what do you want?"

"Joo-yah, I'm not feel good."

"Should I get you some water?" I asked, walking toward the door.

"Joo-yah, don't leave me. Don't leave me."

Weeping into his pillow, my father begged me not to leave him. He said none of it was his fault. The doctors said she couldn't have any children, and then Min Joo came along, my crying Min Joo; he said he wanted to see his son, his own flesh and blood.

That night, I returned to my room, stuffed my mouth with a corner of my blanket, and wept because my father, in his stupor, had confessed that the mother who had left me, and whom I had waited and longed for, was not mine.

14

You liked anchovy soup, so I stunk up my hair and the house to cook it for you. You wanted eel, I almost burned down the house smoking it for you. You liked live squid, so I fought with its tentacles to dump them in the *kimchi* for you. I cut them up, dumped them in the stinging red sauce, and they were still moving. You wanted to listen to old Korean songs, so I bought a tape of *"Barley Field," "When We Depart," "The Waiting Heart,"* and *"The Wild Chrysanthemum"* at Korean Korner for you. For weeks I heard, *"Above the sky a thousand feet high, there are some wild geese crying," "Where, along the endless road are you going away from me like a cloud? like a cloud? like a cloud?" "Lonesome with the thoughts of my old days."* I had to eat my corn flakes with crying geese and rivers that flowed with the blood of twenty lovers. You wanted to read a story about rabbits, so I borrowed *The Tales of Peter Rabbit* for you. You liked cowboy movies, so I bought John Wayne videos for you. You liked to garden, so I stole Mrs. Lee's perilla seeds for you. Your help quit on you, so I skipped two weeks' worth of classes to fry shrimp, steam cabbage, boil collard greens, and bake biscuits for you. You liked Angela's mother, so I drove to her store in Southeast D.C. to set up a dinner date for you. You thought you were losing your hearing, so I laid your head on my thigh and removed the wax out of your ears for you.

You sat on the couch. Your feet rested on top of the

table. Your gray eyebrows fell over your drooping lids. On top of your heaving stomach, your hands were folded, and the remote control was balanced on your left thigh. You flipped through the channels when I told you I had grilled the croaker and that my car was up to 9,000 miles. You flipped through the channels when I asked you to show me how to change my oil. Without turning your head to look at me, you said that I had to get under the car, that I would crush my head, that I would die. Too dangerous. You told me to get it done and that it was cheap, as you handed me a twenty-dollar bill from your shorts pocket and walked to the kitchen table to eat your grilled croaker. But it was a Sunday evening. Everything was closed on Sunday evenings, and I could already hear the knocking.

"I can hear the knocking."

You broke off the tail end of the croaker and bit into it, leaving the fin between your thumb and middle finger. You chewed the bones and spit them out. "Knocking? That's something else. Not oil problem."

"Anyway, I need to know how to change my oil."

You sunk your spoon into the rice. "You write anything?"

I lied to you and told you I had written two stories.

"That's it? When you write something big? Write something big for me."

"I am not going to write something big for you. That's impossible."

"What about?"

"What about what?"

"Your stories." Your chopsticks poked the middle

of the croaker. The skin slid off. You'll save the skin for last, right after you've slurped its brains out, after you've sucked its eyes out. Makes you smarter. Makes you see good.

"One's about that woman you told me about. You know, the one who lived on Hae Un Dae Beach with her daughter. And the daughter always wore that black-and-white knit dress with the snowflake patterns?"

"What about them?"

"Well, the daughter grows up and finds a job at a bakery and leaves her mother on the beach."

"That's not true."

"I know. I'm still working on it."

You looked at me, but I stared at the thin layer of grease floating on top of your water. You wanted to call me a liar, but instead you asked, "What about other?"

"It's about your friend who had the two wives. The first one was a little crazy, so he brought in the good-looking second one who sold cosmetics?"

"What about them?"

"The crazy one ends up jumping out of their apartment window on the eleventh floor."

"Didn't happen like that. But sounds good. Second one sell better than first one. Dying at end is good."

"Just show me how to change my oil."

"The first story, that kind don't sell. You need violence. America likes violence." You spit out your bones. "Like this story. I know. Robber breaks into doctor's house with gun. 'Give me your watch, jewelry, money. Give me everything.' Doctor's not home, but doctor daughter's home. She gives him fake diamond ring, fake ruby ring, fake everything. Robber's happy and goes. Robber tries to make money, sees everything's fake and gets mad and goes back to doctor's house, kidnaps doctor's daughter, and puts tattoo snakes on all over her body. So no one marry her because of tattoos."

"People with tattoos get married."

"Not all over body. Korean man don't like tattoos."

"Then they shouldn't get tattoos."

"Man don't get tattoo. Girl gets tattoo because robber puts on her."

"And he thought she would never get married because of the tattoos?"

"Oh yeah. That's true story." The spinach in your teeth moved.

"Here, you've got spinach in your teeth." You waved your hand at the toothpick and dislodged the spinach with your tongue.

"You buy part and oil?"

"Bought part and oil." You pushed yourself away from the table. "Fry croaker next time. Not enough beans in rice. And you boil spinach too long. Too long. Nothing to chew."

I followed you outside to the driveway with my oil filter and bottles of oil. The crickets started making their noise, and you told me to turn on the porch light. I turned on the porch light. You told me to turn on the driveway light. I turned on the driveway light. The moths and gnats flew in circles above your flat top azalea shrubs like they wanted to drill holes in the air. You told me to get the lightbulb with the hook and the long extension cord on it. From basement, not back there. From basement. You hung it on the hood of my car. You told me to get, you know, car has to go up. The red metal things where the car goes up. And brown carpet in garage. Rags in shed. Bucket behind shed. Not that bucket, stupid. Flat bucket to go under car.

"There is no flat bucket behind the shed."

"What's this?"

"It's a triangular basin. It's not a bucket. Buckets are cylinders and have handles on them."

You threw the bucket under the deck, slapped your right calf, and mumbled something about hell and the mosquitos that surrounded you.

You stood in front of my car. The armholes of your tank top were stretched out showing your chest. Your plaid shorts hung underneath your round hard belly, and your socks were pulled to your knees. You waved the four fingers of your right hand to come. Come. Come. Stop. Your head jerked back, and your chin formed another fold of skin, as you burped. Tasting the croaker again, you licked your lips and swallowed. The crickets screamed from your garden. The street-lights came on, and the mosquitos gathered underneath their light. Slowly, you kneeled and pushed yourself with your slippered feet underneath my car.

Your back rested on the piece of the brown carpet that used to cover the family room, wall to wall. One inch padding underneath. Every step, our feet used to sink in, and our toes would grip the standing fibers. You used to yell, "Take off shoes! Take off shoes!" at my friends, and they would run across the carpet with embarrassment, cheeks turning pink, and leave their shoes at the front door.

The lilac bush collared the driveway light, making it look like a groomed poodle standing still in an angle of your triangular garden. In front of the light, a rock with the glowing "3309" in white paint. The left side was lined with azalea bushes like four green basketballs growing out of white pebbles. The right side was lined with pine trees that looked like four green miniature teepees. And the side that lined the edge of our front porch, more azalea bushes, but with flat tops like coffins. In the center of it all, the stump of the magnolia tree you chopped down because its leaves were clogging up our gutter. The Spanish moss you had planted surrounded the stump and began to climb the rotting bark.

You placed the basin underneath the spout and unscrewed the blue filter. The black oil poured out onto your fingers, then into the basin. You wiped your hand with an old sock.

"Where you drive your car? Oil is so black."

"Let me do it. I'll catch the oil."

"Don't touch anything. Your hands get dirty. Keep clean hands."

"I don't care if my hands get dirty."

"Keep clean hands."

"What do I need clean hands for?"

"Keep clean hands to write."

The oil dripped into the basin. Standing up and wiping your hands on the sock, you told me about Miryang. Miryang. Miryang. Miryang. I know. That was the village you grew up in and in that village was a bridge you had to cross to get to school in your bare feet even during the winter because your father bought you only one pair of shoes on New Year's Day, which you stuffed in your pocket so that the soles wouldn't wear out. And when the soles wore out, you nailed wood to the bottom of your shoes, but the wood gave you splinters, so you poured soil in your shoes; it felt just like walking in a fertilized field.

I know about the tree that stood next to the well. The tree that you climbed and napped on. The tree from which you saw the well holding the floating village virgin. The tree under which the village grandmothers peeled potatoes. You've already told me about the man with three teeth and eight and a half fingers who ran the village grocery. Who would get so drunk by early afternoon that he'd give you a bottle of *soju* rather than the bottle of vinegar your mother was waiting for at home. I've already seen the soybean woman rolling her cart along the dirt road through the village. The chestnut woman who strung her roasted nuts on strands of her own hair. The cows bumping into each other within the fence. The stink of manure in your mother's garden. The stink of sewage when it rained. The rice-grinding factory where you met your mother-in-law. You've already told me about the girl with no eyes marrying the man with no ears. About hiding from your father when school tuition day came around because he'd make you work in the field. Yes, I can hear him yelling, "What good is school? What good is school? Go work in the field." I know about how he broke your watch on your wedding day trying to strike you across the face. It was your engagement watch from Mother. You didn't know then, did you? That she would leave us. Why don't you tell me the truth? Is she my mother or isn't she? How else could she have so easily left me? Why don't you just tell me the truth? I already know about your brother reading books by candlelight underneath a quilt that caught on fire. You don't have to tell me about your sister who was knuckled by your mother so often that she had a dent on the right side of her head and lost her mind and is now steaming rice and boiling potato roots for Buddhist monks. Don't you think I remember the apples, eggs, chestnuts, persimmons you stole and hid in the hole you dug and lined with rocks next to the village manure pile? You don't have to start singing about trying to forget, trying to forget. About walking to the sea sands from day to day. About how summer has gone; fall has gone; now the cold winter in the sea. Abba, I know the women divers searching for clams have disappeared. Stop it. Stop singing about trying to forget, trying to forget by walking to the sea sands from day to day.

You closed my hood, and I drove my car down. You picked weeds out of your garden while I put everything back in its place. You waited for me. When I walked to the door, you followed me in, saying, "Joo-yah, remember when you sing *Bbo gook bbo gook bbo gook seh?"*

"Abba, I don't remember that song."

"You remember."

"I don't."

"Bbo gook bbo gook bbo gook seh . . ."

"Abba, I told you I don't remember. Stop it." You

saw me roll my eyes. Your shoulders jerked back. Three folds of skin formed on your chin. You removed your gray hat and scratched your bald head. Your belly grew as you took your breath.

When I walked upstairs, I heard you say, "No matter how bad my father treat me, I never talk like that. Never walk away like that."

I did not hear the usual sounds of the evening. No commercials from the television, no faucet running, no flush of the toilet every two hours, no refrigerator door opening and closing. I did not hear you speaking to Angela's mother in Korean on the phone. *How was business today? Did you do well? How's Angela? I sent you a letter. Did you get my letter? Ahn Joo? She's writing her stories upstairs.* You didn't call me down to make you Sullok tea or peel apple-pears or listen to your stories about kite fights, crispy grasshopper legs, and midnight runs to the village nurse's window where she changed her clothes in the light. I waited for you to call me down, but I heard you climb the stairs, pass my room, and shut your door.

That night I opened my window. The passing cars on Morning Glory Way were the first sounds I noticed when we moved here. Never heard cars whiz by like that tucked away on the fifth floor of our apartment at the end of Burning Rock Court. I thought a family room with fireplace, living room, dining room, a country kitchen, basement, four bedrooms, two and a half baths were too much for us, but you said, "Future. Future. Think about future." So I thought about the future when I entered junior high and high school, and I raised my hand when I didn't understand how rectification, amplification, and oscillation worked in explaining electrical currents or why bromine was called bromine. I raised my hand when I had to go to the bathroom or if the boys in my lab group were eating all the peanuts we had to weigh. I memorized Xe for Zenon, At for Astatine, Pb for Lead; postulate number one, the points on a line can be paired with the real numbers in such a way that any two points can have zero and one; postulate number two, if B is between AC, then AB plus BC equals AC; Il a mis le café / Dans la tasse / Il a mis le lait / Dans la tasse de café. . . . I thought about the future as I stood in front of Mr. Huggins's geography class and recited Alabama, Alaska, Arizona, Arkansas, California, Colorado, Connecticut, Delaware, Florida . . . all the states in alphabetical order within two minutes. I thought about the future as I bowed and received my classmates' applause.

When future, future, future finally came, the walls of our house were too close together, the ceilings weren't high enough, the floors weren't low enough, and I needed more bedrooms.

Across the street, Mrs. Goode's dogs panted, barked, and jingled the fence. The crickets were going mad, and birds screamed at each other. Mrs. Cutler's high heels tapped quickly against the sidewalk. Mrs. Winehart's car wouldn't start. The phone next door rang. The lawn mower roared. When the wind blew, the screen of my window rattled.

I went downstairs to prepare your tea. As I waited for the water to boil, I shut my eyes tight. But the mahogany bookcase you built when I entered college, the television case for which you hand-carved the legs, the pine coffee table with the drawers that took weeks to make, the kitchen cabinets you stained, the round breakfast table you made me stand on when you cut out its top, the hardwood floors you laid in the living room, and the oyster white kitchen walls you painted stared at me, even behind my closed lids. I could let the water boil and all this wood go up in flames.

Light came from underneath your door. I put down the tray, knocked, and slowly turned the handle when I didn't hear your usual, "Uh." On my hands and knees, I slid the tray into your room.

You had already spread your quilt out on the middle of the floor. Your box of a pillow on the right side. Bare windows. Empty walls except for the photograph of Mother's blurry face tacked above the breakfast-in-bed table. I could never make out what she looked like in that picture. Her hair blew in her face, and she looked like she was shaking her head. No, No. Like she didn't want to be photographed with all those pigeons. A tape player and a digital clock on top of the same table. Underneath, a shoebox of tapes. A pile of three red floor mats in the opposite corner. You sat under the window and fanned yourself.

"Open the window if you're hot."

"Too much noise outside."

You lifted your chin and asked, "What tea did you make?"

"You know, the usual. Sullok tea."

"I thought you make ginseng with honey."

"Why would I make ginseng?"

You reached over for the tray and pulled it to the

edge of your quilt. "Because you want to say something important to me." You said it slowly. You wanted to get all the words in the right order.

With legs crossed and hands folded, you sat in the center of your quilt and waited for me to tell you. I wanted to pour your tea and join you, but I remained on your wooden floor near the door.

In Korean you asked, *"Ahn Joo-yah, what is it?"*

I wanted to tell you that I needed you to tell me about the princess-weaver and her lover, the cowherder, who met at the bank of the River of Heaven every year. How was it that they fell in love? Why did the king separate them? How is it that they meet every year?

Or that I had written a story about your first visit to your grandfather's grave. Fake pink azaleas in a tin can in front of the tombstone. That I had gotten everything down. Your pouring *soju* on the mound. Your peeling a banana and leaving it there for him to eat. Your pulling the weeds off the mound and saying a prayer about how you wanted to be good. Your finishing your prayer and getting up to go, thinking that he would never have known if you had come or gone. Your picking up the banana and eating it. And on your way out, your thinking about how your grandfather died. About how your father never took him to the hospital. If they had opened his stomach, they would have seen the disease, and he would have lived another year. I wanted to tell you that I had gotten everything down. Even the rosebushes that grew like vines on the gate. The fields of rice. The woman who carried a tub of cabbage on her head. The other one who fished for anchovies along the ditch in her rubber gloves. And that I had ended the story with you walking past the two women, leaving the graveyard, and thinking about how you didn't have enough *wons* to buy the dog soup at the end of the road.

Instead, in my best Korean I said, *"Abba, I can't stay here any longer."*

You reached over, poured the tea, and sipped it. Your gold caps sparkled from the corners of your smile. You placed your cup on the wooden saucer and rested your head on your pillow. I opened your closet, pulled out the light blue blanket with the butterfly patterns, and spread it out over you.

"Ahn Joo-yah, I don't need a blanket tonight. It's hot." Your eyes were closed. You pretended to sleep.

"Abba, I'm sorry."

"It's all right. I'm not going to die from the heat."

I folded the blanket away from you and left it at your feet.

"Ahn Joo-yah, leave the tea when you go."

"I know."